YAKUP ALMELEK

THE BUSINESSMAN

İstanbul–Zürich–London

YAKUP ALMELEK

THE BUSINESSMAN

Translated from the Turkish
by Alvin Parmar

ARION
PUBLISHING

Library of Congress Control Number: 2008931683.

AP 002

www.arionpublishing.co.uk

arion@arionpublishing.co.uk

First Published in English, August 2008 - Arion Publishing

30 Amberwood Parkway, Ashland, OH 44805, USA

Address: PK 395   34433 Sirkeci / İSTANBUL – TR

Tel: +90 216 449 56 49

Printed in Turkey by Barış Printing.
Davutpaşa Cad. Güven Sanayi Sitesi C Blok No: 291 Topkapı / İstanbul
Tel: + 90 212 674 85 28

ISBN 978–9944–0709–2–8

The Businessman was published in Turkey in 2007. It was the first of Yakup Almelek's plays to be published, the first play to be published by Arion and the first play that we decided to translate from Turkish to English.

The Businessman has been staged by İzmir Municipal Theatre. So far, Yakup Almelek has had three of his plays performed in Turkey and one of his short stories, *Five Lira a Week*, has been adapted for the cinema.

Yakup Almelek has been active writing plays, marches and articles for his regular column in *Şalom* newspaper for many years and has had a selection of his newspaper articles and short stories published.

In *The Businessman*, Yakup Almelek tries to share with the reader some of the experience that he has gained from being in business himself and the lessons that he has learned. He does this, though, not in a dry, didactic way, but rather by bringing to life the dilemmas that we all face in the form of a play that makes us question our priorities and makes us ask ourselves if we too have been tilting at windmills all this time.

Arion Publishing

About the author:

Yakup Almelek was born in Ankara in 1936 and attended Ankara College. After finishing high school there, he moved to Istanbul with his family in 1955. He graduated from the School of Economics and Commerce in İstanbul.

Starting from fifth grade, he would work during every summer holiday. Among other things, he worked as an accountant's assistant and tried his hand at marketing. He learnt much from the experience that all these summer jobs gave him, and many of the incidents he lived through then, incidents which reflect human nature and Turkey in those days, appear in his articles and short stories.

In 1967, he founded his own company, now in its forty-first year.

Ever since middle school, alongside his professional life, he has indulged his inner life: *reading and writing...* He has written poetry, verse, marches, stories, newspaper articles and plays. While he was still at school, one of his articles won a competition and was published in *Cumhuriyet* newspaper. In the years that followed, more of his writing appeared in the newspaper. He now writes a regular column for *Şalom*.

One of his short stories has been turned into a film and three of his plays – *The Businessman, The Awakening* and *The Governess* – have been staged.

Yakup Almelek is married with two children.

To my Father,

You are the one who imparted a love of books in me. From you I learnt that literature and music contain the priceless truths of life.

I can never repay you.

Rest in peace.

Characters

Aydın Tuna, a 60 to 65 year old successful businessman.

İnci San, his secretary. A pretty woman aged from 40 to 50.

The Doctor, a mild-mannered man, also 60 to 65 years old.

Çelik Tuna, Aydın Tuna's elder son, 23 years old.

Erhan Tuna, Aydın Tuna's younger son, 20 years old.

Luigia Giorgio, a pretty woman aged from 30 to 35.

Vittorio Giorgio, her younger brother, 16 to 18 years old.

ACT ONE – Scene One

Aydın Tuna's study. There is a desk on the left of the stage. In front of the desk, there are two armchairs and a sofa. On the right, a meeting table. There are chairs around the table, and, on the right or the left, a bookcase. On the wall hang one or two paintings, and two sculptures stand on the floor. On the side table next to the desk, there is a computer. Papers and files lie on the desk. A few telephones. A sixty to sixty-five-year old man is sunk in one of the armchairs; he has put his feet up on the desk, and he is talking on the telephone. He is a successful businessman. He has a worn-out appearance. Sometimes he becomes lost in what is being said; sometimes he is wide-awake and alert...

Aydın Tuna:	(*On the telephone, cheerfully*) So, they're in a pretty bad way, huh? Well, let's just stand back and let them carry on until they really hit rock bottom. Then we'll step in. What are the partners supposed to do with a factory that's not making a profit? Soon they'll start selling off their shares.
Voice on the phone:	(*Factory Manager*) Sir, as your factory manager, I'm keeping a close eye on their situation, as well as doing my actual job. And I'm happy to tell you that some of the partners have even been offering their shares to us.
Aydın Tuna:	(*On his feet and walking round the room*) Don't rush into it; don't look too enthusiastic either. We'll sit back and wait for them to go bankrupt.
Voice on the phone:	Even the price they're asking for today isn't that bad; it could easily bail us out.

11

Aydın Tuna:	In six months, they'll be grateful for half of it.
Voice on the phone:	Very well, Sir.
Aydın Tuna:	We'll buy up the partners' shares, one by one, softly softly, without anyone noticing. And in that way, we'll be rid of a major competitor for good.
Voice on the phone:	And that's exactly what we're hoping for, Sir.
Aydın Tuna:	Follow my instructions to the letter. Don't do anything off your own bat. We'll destroy them with our own intelligence and tactics. Don't make a wrong move. I don't want any slip-ups.
Voice on the phone:	Of course not, Sir.
Aydın Tuna:	Let the price of our products fall. Let's say about thirty percent. Make payments easier for our customers. For example, give them long repayment plans. That way, sales will fall even lower.
Voice on the phone:	But Sir, in that case, we'll be making big losses too.
Aydın Tuna:	So be it, losses like that aren't going to destroy us, but they'll leave our competitor in a very tight situation. And after a while, we'll have them right where we want them. And when there's only us left, then we'll raise our prices again.
Voice on the phone:	Of course, Sir.
Aydın Tuna:	And I want a progress report each week. Keep me up to date on the latest developments.

Voice on the phone:	Very good, Sir. (*He puts the phone down*)
Aydın Tuna:	(*To himself*) God, that manager's as thick as two short planks! But, then again, people like him are just what we need for this job... You can never trust people who are too clever.

(*İnci San, the secretary, enters. She is a pretty woman aged 40–50 wearing a plain dress.*)

İnci San:	I've got some bad news for you, Mr Tuna. The Ministry's response about the incentives and tax breaks is a no.
Aydın Tuna:	What? They've refused? Who from the Ministry signed it?
İnci San:	Ahmet, the undersecretary. Here's what he said to me on the phone, (*imitating the undersecretary's voice*) "Oh, and do send my regards to Mr Tuna. Tell him he should think again about riding our wave to the top. Whatever he does, it'll have to be by his own efforts."
Aydın Tuna:	Well, well, well, so that's what Ahmet the undersecretary has decreed, is it? Look, here's what we'll do: get the news out to our writer. Let him start an anti-government campaign. There's still some time to go before the elections; still, their day shall come.
İnci San:	Come, come, aren't we being a little hasty?
Aydın Tuna:	What do you mean?

İnci San: Well, I think that if they don't give us the necessary permission, we should let on to the minister
that we're going to *start* a smear campaign... They
don't want to see you up against them. And they
don't want to run the risk that you will. But if, in
spite of all that, there's still no decision in three
months, then we'll steam into publication. An eye
for an eye, a tooth for a tooth...

Aydın Tuna: OK then, İnci, that's fine with me, too. Let's do it
your way.

İnci San: You know, Mr Tuna, you told me last month that
you wanted to go into politics. A big businessman
dabbling in politics... And they might applaud, or
they might boo... Your heart is set on the Ministry
of Finance, isn't it? As a first step, I mean...

Aydın Tuna: Yes, you could say that.

İnci San: Well, I think we should wait a little. I mean like
this: let the decision for the factory come. Then,
let's start building. We'll import the machinery on a
loan from the Central Bank and not pay any VAT.
Then we'll meet up with the party leaders and see
what the lie of the land is. Who's going to offer you
what... I mean, before you join any of the parties,
you have to have at least some kind of guarantee
of a ministry.

Aydın Tuna: You're a very intelligent woman, İnci. Whatever
would I do without you?

İnci San: And you taught me everything I know, Mr Tuna. Right here in this holding company, my school. (*The sound of the switchboard comes from the internal phone*) Your doctor has arrived, Sir.

Aydın Tuna: (*Cheerfully*) Show him in straight away.

(*İnci San exits*)

Scene Two

(The Doctor enters. He is a gentle, mild-mannered man of a similar age to Aydın Tuna. As soon as Aydın Tuna sees him, he gets up and hugs him.)

Aydın Tuna:	Welcome, my dear friend. I was beginning to miss you. If I don't hear your voice for a week, I really do start to get worried.
The Doctor:	I'm here about something very serious. We have to talk.
Aydın Tuna:	I'm listening, fire away.
The Doctor:	You know how seven days ago... (*The telephone rings; the Doctor stops talking and waits*)
Voice on the phone:	(*The switchboard*) Your representative in Japan is calling, sir.
Aydın Tuna:	Put him through, put him through. (*He turns to the Doctor*) It won't take long: I'll keep it short.
Voice on the phone:	(*The representative in Japan*) How are you, Sir?
Aydın Tuna:	(*Impatiently*) Fine, fine, let's get straight to the point, I'm listening.
Voice on the phone:	The Japanese don't want to make a deal. They say our conditions are too tough; they can't possibly accept them.

Aydın Tuna:	Let them say what they want. They're so sly. It's a trick to see the lay of the land. Keep your cool; don't look to desperate.
Voice on the phone:	They say they've had other bids from our country, other more reasonable bids.
Aydın Tuna:	(*Laughing*) Oh, so they've had other bids, have they? Not to worry, if we're not part of it, the others won't get involved. They're afraid. Mind you don't go making any concessions, now; just wait. Call me in three days at the latest.
Voice on the phone:	Very good, Sir.

(*He hangs up*)

Aydın Tuna:	(*Looking at the Doctor*) We're getting into the electronics industry with the Japanese. A joint venture... It's big, very big. We'll be the only ones in the whole of Europe, the only ones. My friend, we're about to set up our fortieth company!
The Doctor:	(*Impatiently*) I'm so happy for you. Congratulations. Now, listen up.
Aydın Tuna:	I'm all ears. Go ahead.
The Doctor:	Now, you remember you came to me a week ago...

(*The telephone rings*)

Voice on the phone:	(*The switchboard*) It's London office, Sir.

Aydın Tuna:	(*Turning to the Doctor*) Give me a couple of minutes, will you? I'll get rid of this one immediately. (*To the switchboard*) Put them through, love.
Voice on the phone:	(*The London office*) Sir, the Middle East export link is pretty much OK. There's just been one little hiccough. There's going to be an additional outlay. The goods we gave them were a little substandard. At least, that's what they're saying.
Aydın Tuna:	If that's what they're saying, then they're lying! Get it sorted, love. Tug on their heart strings a little. Pull your finger out.
Voice on the phone:	They're waiting. I told them I couldn't decide without talking to you first.
Aydın Tuna:	You did the right thing, yes, the right thing. Start at one percent and go up as far as three. No receipt, of course. Pay him under the counter. Embrace him behind the curtain.
Voice on the phone:	Alright, Sir, I think I should be able to solve the problem like that. I'll let you know the outcome tomorrow at the latest.

(*He hangs up*)

Aydın Tuna:	(*To himself as if he has forgotten that the Doctor is also there*) What a cheating cow! She'll give two, but say she's given three just to keep one for herself, but what do I know, when it comes to finishing off a job, she's an expert tightrope walker. (*Suddenly*

	remembering the Doctor) I'm sorry; I've kept you waiting, go ahead.
Doctor:	(*Patiently*) You know how we had some tests done, when you had your full check up... (*The telephone rings*)
Voice on the phone:	(*The switchboard*) Mr Tuna, it's the manager of the Doğu Factory, and he says it's very, very important; he really needs to speak to you.
Aydın Tuna:	(*Looks at the Doctor and shrugs his shoulders. The Doctor laughs and motions for him to speak*) OK then, love, put him through.
Voice on the phone:	(*Doğu Factory*) Sir, it's Adnan. Your secretary said you were in a meeting, but it's just there's something I really have to tell you...
Aydın Tuna:	(*Interrupting him*) What? A meeting? Ah, yes: I have a guest. Very well, then, make it quick.
Voice on the phone:	Sir, the unions are threatening us. They're going to go on strike. They want an eighty-percent pay rise.
Aydın Tuna:	(*Shouting*) Are they out of their tiny, little minds? Unbelievable! Why eighty percent? Why not sixty?
Voice on the phone:	The cost of living, something called inflation, price rises, blah, blah, blah...
Aydın Tuna:	Are we the ones raising prices? What are we supposed to do about it? They should go and take it

out on the incompetent government. It's the prime minister they should be talking to, not me!

Voice on the phone: If you were to meet with the trades unionists, maybe you could convince them...

Aydın Tuna: (*Shouting*) There's no way I'm coming over there. And I don't want them over here, either. Go and tell this to your union leaders: If there's going to be a strike, then there'll be a lock out, too. So they shouldn't be giving me any aggro. I'll show them who I am. I'll close the whole bloody factory down!

Voice on the phone: But, Sir, they're really digging their heels in.

Aydın Tuna: Put a couple of spies among the workers. Work out who the ringleaders are. Then find some excuse to make heads roll.

Voice on the phone: The situation's critical. They've given us an ultimatum. They'll down tools in a week; they're deadly serious about that.

Aydın Tuna: Keep them sweet. Distract them until the end of the season. And then, we'll give them a maximum of fifty percent. If we get rid of their leaders first, their voices won't be as loud. Look, if we give them more than fifty, it could harm the factory. Do you understand?

Voice on the phone: I'll call you again tomorrow, Sir.

Aydın Tuna: (*Angrily*) Look, my friend, you're the factory manager, aren't you? So show us what you're made of! And if you're not up to it, tell me now, and I'll send someone from here who is. (*He hangs up*)

(*The Doctor has been following the conversations carefully; as soon as the phone is hung up, he turns to Aydın Tuna*)

The Doctor:	Can you do me a favour? Can you call İnci in here for a moment?
Aydın Tuna:	(*Bemused*) Of course, yes, I'll tell her to come in. (*On the internal phone*) İnci, can you come here for a moment?

(*İnci San enters*)

The Doctor:	(*Speaking to İnci San*) I've got a favour to ask of you, love. As your boss' GP and as this company's doctor, I'm asking you not to put any calls through from anyone, starting from now and for the next thirty minutes, that's thirty little minutes. I don't care if it's some state dignitary, or some influential CEO of a big holding; whoever it is, you'll tell them that Mr Tuna is not here for an entire half-hour.

(*Aydın Tuna starts to laugh and turns to İnci San*)

Aydın Tuna:	It's OK, İnci, do exactly as the doctor orders.

(*İnci San gives instructions to the switchboard from the internal phone, and as she is leaving the room:*)

The Doctor:	İnci, I didn't get round to asking you how your husband is. Is he any better?

İnci San:	He's improved quite a lot, Doctor. He's at home convalescing now. He's uncomfortable, but it'll get better, of course.
The Doctor:	Give him my regards. If you want anything, don't hesitate to ask.
İnci San:	Thank you, Doctor. We'll never forget all you've done for us. Thank you very much. (*İnci San exits*)
Aydın Tuna:	(*Surprised*) What was wrong with her husband? Was he ill? She didn't tell me. Maybe I was abroad.
The Doctor:	Didn't you know? The poor man had a heart attack. You're so busy she never has a chance to tell you anything personal.
Aydın Tuna:	You're right, but you can see what it's like, how much work I have.
The Doctor:	(*Sternly*) Yes, I certainly can. You're really quite something.
Aydın Tuna:	For half an hour, there'll be no calls, no visitors, no nothing. A meaningful silence... Now, my friend, tell me why you're here. Wait, wait, don't start just yet; I've got something to ask you. How's the construction of the old people's home going? There isn't enough money, is there? Tell me how much you need and I'll write you out a cheque for it straight away. Let's sort it out. Then we'll get onto the real topic...
The Doctor:	Let's not talk about that now. There's enough

	money. Besides, it's your health that we should be talking about.
Aydın Tuna:	We've been friends since we were fifteen. Fifty years, easily. I've never seen you like this before: so nervous and agitated.
The Doctor:	You know how we had those tests done a week ago... Now, I'm going to be frank with you. The results aren't good, not good at all. (*Aydın Tuna listens impassively, his eyes fixed on a point on the wall*) We sent your blood and the tissue sample we took to three different labs. And the results were all the same. The same data in Istanbul, Geneva and London. And this morning, I consulted two professors from the hospital.
Aydın Tuna:	(*Coolly*) And does this illness have a name? How long have I got left?
The Doctor:	The Lord moves in mysterious ways.
Aydın Tuna:	Are we going to rely on God or on medical science? Or are they both a sham? Now tell me, please, how long have I got left?
The Doctor:	Maybe three, maybe four months. It's a pity that the disease is in its advanced stages. If we had only caught it six months ago, maybe we could have done something. But now it's too late. I would have preferred not to have had to tell you something like this. But what would have been the use? I haven't hidden anything from you because I know how strong you are. And you've got your empire here,

in the economic sense. I thought that if you knew exactly how things stood, you might want to make a few decisions about what will happen after you're gone.

Aydın Tuna: So, three or four months... That's terrible news. What should I be thinking? Should I be saying *après nous, le déluge* and leave everything to its fate, or should I be trying to cram all the changes I see as necessary into three months? The first choice seems more appropriate to my mind. Thank God my mind can still grasp the situation I'm in. Don't tell me what's wrong with me. I can guess. Damn it!

The Doctor: What's that supposed to mean?

Aydın Tuna: Of course, I always knew that one day I'd pass away. You can't deny the inevitability of death. But you never think of a specific time; you never want to remember that one day you'll be gone. To approach the finishing line in a race you've been running for years, finally to taste life along with death... That's how I am at the moment. Think about it, my friend; what kind of painful game is this? And who's playing it with me? Who's conned me, fleeced me, stripped me bare? Who pushed me into this ridiculous struggle? What's the reason for me being ill? I'm sure it's some kind of brain malfunction. If I have a mind, why didn't it warn me not to enter this God-forsaken whirlpool? How well it kept me occupied with this lust for wealth! Damn it...

The Doctor: Wait a minute, Aydın, don't blame it on your work ethic. That would be unfair.

Aydın Tuna:	Is the brain that covered my life in fake glitter really mine? Damn it, damn it, damn it!... What sins have I committed to deserve this? To slowly wither away and be extinguished in pain and suffering... Waiting for the inevitable end is worse than the end itself. But no, my friend, no... Why am I blaming my mind? Why can't it be God who concocted this pain for me, who set up this hell? My illness is Satan's partnership with God.
The Doctor:	You know, I wish I'd never told you. I wish I'd waited for the inevitable end to come of its own accord.
Aydın Tuna:	No, no, it's better this way. (*Stopping for a moment*) Come, let's rethink it. Let's turn pessimism into optimism. I wonder if I'm not misinterpreting a God-given opportunity? How many people know their end is nigh three months beforehand? Who knows? Maybe this information is a gift of fate? A priceless gift for one of God's beloved creatures? It has woken me up from a deep sleep. And now, sleep has been banished from my eyes. Look into them, I've only got twelve more weeks to live... Now I have two lovers... One is life; the other is death... First, I'll make love to life; then I'll be death's. Lucky old me...
The Doctor:	I feel so helpless; what can I do to comfort you?
Aydın Tuna:	I'm a good businessman, my friend. I'm closed to daydreaming and misunderstanding. But as for reality, how ever ugly its face might be, I'm open to it right to the bitter end. Is there such a big difference

25

between them? To die in a car accident or fall victim to a heart attack or – I won't use that dirty word – to be consumed with the anguish of an upheaval in the metabolic system... All ends are equal, in the end.

The Doctor: I almost want *you* to console me now.

Aydın Tuna: We've been friends for fifty years. We were in the same class at middle school and high school. After high school, I threw myself into the business world; you continued on to medical school, and became a doctor. We remained friends. Riding the crest of a friendship that has kept growing.

The Doctor: If it hadn't been for you, I wouldn't even have been able to go to medical school. What you've done for me is tucked away in the most beautiful corner of my heart. I can never repay my debt to you. I was an orphan. It was impossible for me to go on to medical school. I had no income at all. Every month, you would come to the dorm and leave me some money to meet my expenses. Those four years are a burden I will never be able to forget, let alone repay.

Aydın Tuna: You're a big, bad professor now. If I've been able to add a few grains of salt to the soup, then I am the one who should be saying thank you.

The Doctor: Remember how you went to primary school in London? What great English you could speak! I would follow you around trying to get you to teach me the tenses, you know past tense, present tense...

Aydın Tuna:	I was proud to do it. I wasn't a good student in middle school or high school. English was my lifebelt. In some lessons, I would do translations for the teachers to get myself out of hot water.
The Doctor:	If now I can sort of get by in English, then that's all down to you.
Aydın Tuna:	No, it's not; someone with your perseverance could even learn Chinese. (*As if wanting to change the subject*) Do you remember when you were studying at medical school, you forced me to go to a concert with you?
The Doctor:	How could I forget? You used to say, "How can you give up your Saturday afternoon for a concert?"
Aydın Tuna:	That's right, but when I heard that there'd be girls there too, I accepted.
The Doctor:	And at the first one, what a coincidence! There we were, sitting next to two brunettes. And how we clapped the orchestra, you know, just to show we knew a little about music!
Aydın Tuna:	Yes but they started to sweat when we asked them out to dinner with the both of us, remember?
The Doctor:	You were the one who invited them. What was it they said? (*Imitating a girl's voice*) "We're engaged so leave us alone." And let's see if you can remember what you said to them.

Aydın Tuna:	(*Clearing his throat once or twice*) "Well you're missing out on a golden opportunity, ladies. My friend here is going to be a famous doctor, and, as for me, in twenty years, I'll be a trillionaire businessman. I'm sure that your fiancés are nothing compared to us." That's exactly what I said.
The Doctor:	Well, that's amazing. Even today, your memory is as strong as mine. Anyway, tell me, my friend, what was the girl's reply?
Aydın Tuna:	(*Clearing his throat once or twice, and imitating a girl's voice*) "You've overheated; the weather's hot; you should take a cold shower." (*They both burst out laughing*) OK, well, here's another question to test your memory. What was the first piece we listened to at that concert?
The Doctor:	Ah, what was it now? I've got it! Liszt's Second Hungarian Rhapsody.
Aydın Tuna:	And the second?
The Doctor:	Ulvi Cemal Erki's Köçekçesi.
Aydın Tuna:	OK well, think about the third piece. The first one after the interval...
The Doctor:	It was something by a Russian. Now what was it? I've got it! Rimsky-Korsakov's Scheherazade.
Aydın Tuna:	And tell me, what was Scherezade about?

The Doctor:	Call off your dogs... How am I supposed to know what it was about?
Aydın Tuna:	If only you'd listened instead of eyeing up the brunette sitting next to you. The conductor explained the piece briefly before playing it. I'll tell you as much as I can remember. "Shahriyar, the king of Persia, thinks that his wife is cheating on him and wants to take his anger out on all women. He decides he will sleep with a different woman every night and have her killed the next morning. The first victim is to be a really pretty girl by the name of Scheherezade. At midnight, the king, tired and exhausted with lust, said to Scheherezade, 'Say your prayers; if you want to know why, it's because your beautiful head will be parting company with your body before long.' Scherezade said, 'Your Majesty, please give me a chance.' The king couldn't understand what he could grant her. Scheherazade said, 'Death is darkness; life is light; the splendour of daylight is much more magnificent than the night. I'm going to tell you a story. If you like it, then let me eyes stay open until tomorrow evening. If you don't like my tale, give your order to the executioner, get it over with. He admired the girl's spirit and told her to start straight away. The girl started to tell such a story that the king was spellbound. The sky started to become light, but the story wasn't over. 'Your Majesty,' said the girl, 'let's continue this evening.' In all, the stories continued for a thousand and one nights. Each night, a story saved the beautiful Scheherezade from death. In the end, the king admitted the girl to his harem, and they lived happily ever after."

The Doctor:	Yes, I do remember that! Didn't we read that story in our literature lessons?
Aydın Tuna:	If we had a memory race, yours would lap mine. But you see how it works... The king grants the right to live: one day for one story. Even God doesn't dispense his justice so generously. You've read a lot of religious books in your time, so you should know. Azrael is God's assistant, isn't he?
The Doctor:	You're trying to start a quarrel about your relationship with God. Do you think they write that sort of thing in books?
Aydın Tuna:	Never mind, anyway, I'll learn everything about the other side in three or four months. For example, why am I very rich, but other people aren't?
The Doctor:	You're very intelligent, and you make the most of your opportunities.
Aydın Tuna:	OK, then, but why aren't other people as intelligent as me, or why can't they make the most of opportunities? So many people live in Turkey. From a financial perspective, you can count on the fingers of one hand the number of people who are as successful as me. Why is that?
The Doctor:	Let's just say it's coincidence.
Aydın Tuna:	If you entrust justice to the lottery, will anyone have any faith in religious and legal institutions? For example, does religion bring justice to society? How successful are laws in providing justice? Where does

my right to be this rich come from? But anyway, I don't have to worry myself about that at the moment. In ninety or a hundred days or anyway, some time in the near future, I'll be in a deep sleep where I'll be able to grasp the depth of the subject fully. Why? Because the dead know everything.

The Doctor: (*Looking at his watch*) Aydın, your accounts manager is ill. He called; I'll go and see him – hopefully it's nothing too serious – and I'll pop back.

Aydın Tuna: He's very good with public finance. He's very important to our holding. (*As if remembering something*) But anyway, who cares about our holding? He's a very good person. He's got a wife and kids; he's young and very cultured. Try and do all you can for him.

The Doctor: I will, Aydın. Thanks.

(*As the Doctor says thanks, both of them look at each other lovingly; the Doctor exits; Aydın Tuna goes towards his desk; as he is about to sit down, he gets up as if startled, and sits in one of the guest chairs; he puts his hands behind his head and leans back*)

Aydın Tuna: (*To himself*) I don't have much time left. The stopwatch isn't going forward anymore; it's counting down. What should I do?

(*He closes his eyes. The lights go down; there is a short piece of music; the lights come back on; Aydın Tuna is still sitting in the same position. The Doctor enters; Aydın Tuna rises to his feet as soon as he sees him*)

Aydın Tuna: What happened? How is he?

The Doctor:	I told him to go to the clinic tomorrow. We'll run an ECG.
Aydın Tuna:	You'll let İnci know the results, won't you?
The Doctor:	Why İnci? Why not you?
Aydın Tuna:	I won't be here. I'm going somewhere this evening.
The Doctor:	Oh, a business meeting or something? Where are you going?
Aydın Tuna:	After you go, I'm going to have a word with İnci. I'm not going to tell her about my illness or that my days are numbered or anything like that. I'm going to make her CEO of the Holding. Then, I'm going to write three letters: one to my sons, one to my wife and one to all the employees in my companies. I'm going to leave them on my desk, hop in a plane, and jet off somewhere. I don't know where I'll be spending the evening.
The Doctor:	I see. Just like that, eh? Well, you've got no money problems, after all. A world trip, is it, eh? Wherever you lay your hat, that's your home, huh? Booze, chicks and while you're at it, a bit of gambling too? Is that what you want to do?
Aydın Tuna:	Not at all. The exact opposite, in fact. I want a place where I can rest.
The Doctor:	Look Aydın, stay here. We'll start treatment. Lasers and that sort of thing, maybe we'll be able to do something. Stay in Istanbul.

Aydın Tuna:

Forget it. We both know it's too late. I haven't listened to you for years. The late diagnosis is completely my own fault. I can't stay in Istanbul. There are a lot more people here who don't like me than people who do. When they hear about my situation, they'll be gloating. Some will come to visit; some will call. False smiles, forced gestures, huge clouds of fake-smelling get-well-soons. I can't cope with it. "Serves him right," they'll be saying to themselves, "he's finally kicking the bucket. All that wealth couldn't help him. Let him try taking his money wherever he's going..."

The Doctor:

(*Interrupting him*) Aydın, you're exaggerating! No one will think that. You're just feeling down at the moment.

Aydın Tuna:

I was feeling down until twenty minutes ago. But not anymore. What I was saying is not just a product of my imagination. I can immediately sense what's going through the hearts and minds of the people I talk to or work with. The times when I'm wrong are few and far between. It's an essential part of being a good businessman. Someone who hasn't got it might be able to open a shop, but could never be the owner of thirty-nine companies and two banks.

The Doctor:

OK, well, stay in Istanbul for a few days at least. You can make your travel plans. Reservations, this and that...

Aydın Tuna:

Actually, that's not the only reason why I want to run away. I'm hungry for freedom. Do you think

I'm free here? I can't even have half an hour off as I please. There's a whole load of worries, things to do, plans, projects... It's as if my brain has been mortgaged and repossessed. The world is full of so many other beautiful things, not just work. I need to think about them. I can't do that here. I'm going to go somewhere where no one knows me. Where the folds of my brain can be purified and cleansed.

The Doctor: What's the point of going abroad? Go to a villa in the south or go to the Black Sea.

Aydın Tuna: Impossible, it wouldn't work. Telephone calls, visits, I'd never be left in peace. I'm going to find a place where no one knows me. I'll be reborn there. I'll make the most of my freedom. Even if it's only for three months, I want to get to know myself better. Who am I? Just a money-making machine? My professional life is finishing as of today. My real freedom starts tomorrow.

The Doctor: I don't understand you. Aren't you free? You used to enjoy working like that.

Aydın Tuna: Mentally, I'm not free; I'm a slave to my job; I'm addicted. I'm condemned to take my work with me wherever I go. Earning money, opening companies, yes, it's fun, but it's superficial. I understood everything better just now. At bottom, it was all just for show. Maybe it was me worrying about having to prove myself. I didn't go to university. Think about my unconscious. I had a hard enough time getting through high school. I didn't get a higher education, but count all my factories. Who else has as many as me? What have you got? OK, so I might have got over my inferiority complex, but at what cost? Was it worth what the price I paid? I looked at my face in the mirror every morning. Pale and gaunt... There was no sign of life apart from two shining eyes. That's what I am today. A sick businessman succumbing to liver cancer.

The Doctor: You said you were going to go somewhere. Where?

Aydın Tuna: Somewhere outside of Turkey... Somewhere in Europe... In four or five hours, wherever there's a plane to. Now wait, now I remember. The night flight, I'll go to London; that's if I can find a seat on the plane, of course...

The Doctor: Are you going to stay there? You've got an export company, a bank and a house in London.

Aydın Tuna: I'll hang around in London for a couple of days. I've got absolutely no intention of popping into the office or the bank. I'm not even going to let them know I'm coming. And I'd appreciate it if you didn't tell anyone about this either. I'm not going to explain anything to my wife or sons. I'll stay in a small hotel.

The Doctor: What do you mean? You'll suddenly disappear, just like that? They'll be worried sick.

Aydın Tuna: If they are, then so much the better. Two loser sons and a gambling wife... Whatever happens, they just idle away their time. Worrying is better than doing nothing.

The Doctor:	And then what are you going to do?
Aydın Tuna:	I'll travel round England for a bit; then I'll go on to Italy.
The Doctor:	Italy? Why Italy?
Aydın Tuna:	Come, my friend, let's take a trip down memory lane. To our middle school days... Who was our art teacher then?
The Doctor:	(*Thinks a little*) Fatma Gündüz.
Aydın Tuna:	That's right; we used to call her "Fatma the Easel". You remember how she used to sit without crossing her legs, and how the boys would sit right opposite her to watch them.
The Doctor:	(*Impatiently*) Yes, but what's that got to do with Italy?
Aydın Tuna:	Fatma the Easel could never praise Italy enough. "Italy," she would say, "is a huge gallery. Adorned with paintings and statues..." I used to like her a lot, and I used to tell myself that when I grew up and was rich, I would definitely go and see Italy. But, unfortunately, I've never had the opportunity. Fatma the Easel's boot-shaped art gallery stayed squarely in my dreams. But now, you see, the opportunity is within reach. If God gives me health, I'll be there in a month.
The Doctor:	But you don't know the language.

Aydın Tuna:	Well, that's even better. Talking can wear you out. I need to relax and listen to myself. I'll say anything important in English, broken French, or, if I have to, with grunts and gestures.
The Doctor:	So you haven't set foot yet in the land of the master pasta chefs... Wait, here's another memory test. Who was our music teacher at middle school?
Aydın Tuna:	Ahmet Ak, a.k.a. Ahmet the Violin... He would make us listen to Paganini from his 78 vinyls. He'd practically have to force us. At first, it used to send me to sleep, but slowly, I began to fall in love with it. He was passionate about Italy, too.
The Doctor:	So was I. I would even have dreams while listening to Vivaldi. Hey, weren't Fatma the Easel and Ahmet the Violin having an affair?
Aydın Tuna:	They definitely were, but I'm keeping my nose out of it; on that topic, they were both experts. They could walk on snow and not leave a footprint. Anyway, live and let live.
The Doctor:	Yes, you could say that.
Aydın Tuna:	You know Vivaldi's Four Seasons: spring, summer, autumn, winter... Well, today, I entered winter. My last season.
The Doctor:	(*Sighing*) Well, where are you going to go after Italy?
Aydın Tuna:	I don't know; we'll see in the morning...

The Doctor:	Where are you going to stay in Italy?
Aydın Tuna:	I'll travel round Venice, Rome, Florence and Sicily. Fatma the Easel's dreams are waiting for me to come and embrace them. It might be a huge disappointment and I might not like them, but if that happens, I'll go somewhere else.
The Doctor:	I'm both your friend and your doctor, and it is my duty to advise you. What if you suddenly take a turn for the worse?
Aydın Tuna:	I've thought about that. I'm taking my mobile phone with me, but I'll keep it switched off. If I fall ill or don't feel well, I'll call you. Even if you're up to your elbows in blood, hop on the first plane. If the flight times aren't convenient, have them rent out a jet.
The Doctor:	Come on now, forget about this flight of fancy. Don't leave Turkey; don't go off like that.
Aydın Tuna:	Impossible. I don't want to die in my homeland, but my final wish is to be buried in my homeland. I'm not in for dying in Turkey, but I am in for being buried in Istanbul. You're the only one I want to be at my side as I lie dying.
The Doctor:	So be it.
Aydın Tuna:	Oh, before I forget, let me ask you something. How is the construction of the old people's home going?

The Doctor:	It's going well, thanks; it's almost finished. We've started decorating the inside.
Aydın Tuna:	Do you need any money? Just tell me, I'll give you it immediately.
The Doctor:	No, we're fine, thanks. We have enough.
Aydın Tuna:	To set up a foundation and build an old people's home is so philanthropic. And you're the one who designed and implemented the whole thing... They will have TVs, won't they?
The Doctor:	Of course. We're going to install a TV almost as big as a cinema screen in the living room.
Aydın Tuna:	But there's a whole load of channels. Is everyone going to watch the same channel?
The Doctor:	Well, what else can we do? We can't put a TV in each room. We'd never be able to manage it.
Aydın Tuna:	Do it; I'll pay. Now let's see, if one TV is about five hundred Euro, that makes twenty-five thousand altogether. I'll write a cheque straight away.
The Doctor:	Wait, Aydın. It's an unnecessary expense; anyone who wants to watch TV can watch it in the living room.
Aydın Tuna:	People who stay in an old people's home have usually already set out on their final journey. They're not as lucky as I am; they don't know when they'll pass away. I'll write that cheque.

(*Writes the cheque*)

The Doctor:	Thank you, on behalf of each resident, one by one...
Aydın Tuna:	I'd like to ask you a favour, if it's possible... When... you know... when I get really bad, when I stop being myself, when the pain becomes too much, could you help me on my way with an injection.
The Doctor:	Aydın, it would hurt me less to stick that needle in my own arm. Don't ask that from me. You are more than a friend or a brother to me. If I do that, won't my hands offend me? Wouldn't I want those hands to be broken?
Aydın Tuna:	Alright, alright, I'd forgotten how tender-hearted you are.
Internal Telephone:	(*The switchboard*) Mr Tuna, the Doctor is with you, isn't he? They're calling from the hospital; something urgent has cropped up; they want him to come immediately.
The Doctor:	Aydın, I have to go. I know whatever I say won't make you change your mind. You've always had a stubborn streak. But call me often at least.
Aydın Tuna:	Look, I'm only going to call you if my situation gets really bad. If I'm well, you'll hear nothing from me. And there's another favour I'd like to ask from you. Have a word with those colleagues of yours you consulted in the hospital. Tell them not to talk about

my illness with anyone. Just like lawyers, doctors should keep secrets too, shouldn't they?

The Doctor:

Don't worry; just now when I was upstairs, I called them just to make sure. And anyway, apart from me, only two other professors know about your condition.

Aydın Tuna:

Anyway, you go now, you don't want to be late. (*They embrace; both of them are making an effort to hold back the tears. The Doctor exits; Aydın Tuna watches him leave through the door with astonishment, sighs and wipes his eyes. To the internal phone*) İnci, could you come here a moment?

Scene Three

(*İnci San enters*)

Aydın Tuna:	İnci, how many years have you been working here?
İnci San:	It'll be thirty years this year.
Aydın Tuna:	If you can't confide your troubles in me, I'll never be able to forgive myself. I think that I'm a very selfish boss. Your husband had an operation, and I didn't know anything about it. Am I really one of those terrible people who only think about themself and their work? Please, judge me. Am I really that kind of person?
İnci San:	You are the perfect businessman. The best one I can think of. Professional life is a completely different world. Every company has its own problems. My husband's heart attack is just a drop in the ocean.
Aydın Tuna:	If you'd said that yesterday, I could have agreed with you, but today I've come to my senses. Nothing is more important than a person and their health. Now tell me, what happened?
İnci San:	My husband had a heart attack three months ago; he was in a critical condition; they operated immediately. Our doctor helped out a lot, too.
Aydın Tuna:	What could have caused his heart attack? Your husband's a thin, athletic man, isn't he?

İnci San:	Yes, he is. I think it was because of unhappiness. The German company he was working for closed down once it'd finished its contract. And it's not easy to find a new job these days. Our house is rented. Four months ago, it was put up for sale. Looking for a house, a job, they're big problems for us.
Aydın Tuna:	Your husband's an engineer. Let's get him a job in one of our factories.
İnci San:	He's a civil engineer. He really loves his job. But he's very proud. He wouldn't want people to think he'd found a job through his wife.
Aydın Tuna:	I see. Well, is there anywhere that he's applied to?
İnci San:	If he could work on site, he could find something, but I don't want him to do that. The summer heat and the winter's cold could destroy his already fragile health.
Aydın Tuna:	Where has he applied to?
İnci San:	The last place was Doğrular Construction. They still haven't replied; we're waiting.
Aydın Tuna:	I know them. They did our third installation. (*To the switchboard*) Love, call Doğrular Construction. Who was the owner, now? OK, I remember, Metin. Put me through to him. Say that I want to speak to him. (*A minute goes by in silence; Aydın Tuna waits motionless, his eyes fixed on a point on the wall. İnci San is standing up, looking at Aydın Tuna lovingly*)

Voice on the phone:	(*The switchboard*) Mr Doğrular is on the line, Sir.
Voice on the phone:	(*Metin*) Hello, Mr Tuna, what can I do for you?
Aydın Tuna:	Actually, I was wondering if you could do me a favour. I heard you were looking for an engineer. I was going to recommend someone to you. I know him well: he's İnci San's husband. But he shouldn't work on the site; he's still recovering from a heart attack. He's very good and he's called Kemal San.
Voice on the phone:	Whatever you say, Mr Tuna; we'll hire him immediately.
Aydın Tuna:	And please, don't tell him I called you. He's very proud.
Voice on the phone:	I won't let on to either Mr or Mrs San that you called me. I'll call the number he wrote on his application form straight away and let him know that he's been hired. He can start in our central office in town.
Aydın Tuna:	Thank you very much. (*He hangs up*) (*Turning to İnci San*) Well, that's that sorted; now, let's move on to the second thing... Didn't you say your house was being put up for sale?
İnci San:	Yes, Mr Tuna, the owner died four months ago. His heirs can't decide how to divide up what he left them.
Aydın Tuna:	You know, I'm totally against this inheritance thing. For someone to own something without putting in the slightest bit of effort, well, it goes against

everything I believe; it's unfair. People who inherit have a headstart on those who don't. It goes against equality. How can we explain the law protecting an unfair system, or, at the very least, rewarding it? Anyway, that's not what we were talking about. How much is it being sold for?

İnci San: Two hundred and fifty thousand Euro!

Aydın Tuna: Is that a good price? Is there a margin for bargaining?

İnci San: They say there isn't.

Aydın Tuna: Well then! İnci, the safe is open; you'll see a small packet on the left; there's three hundred thousand Euro in it. Take the packet and put it in your bag. You know that thug who handles all our real estate business; give him a call and get him to start working on it. The flat you live in should belong to you and your husband.

İnci San: Mr Tuna! How can we repay you?

Aydın Tuna: Don't worry about it. Let's just say it's a present from me. (*İnci San just stands there in amazement*) İnci, don't stand there as if you've seen a ghost. (*İnci San doesn't move; Aydın Tuna goes, comes back with a packet and says tenderly*) Here, take it; I hope you enjoy living in your new home. (*İnci San takes it hesitatingly*)

İnci San: Well, I am surprised: I could never have imagined getting a gift from you. In thirty years, this is the first time you've taken this much interest in something not related to work. I don't know why, but you've become even greater in my eyes. Do you know what the really touching thing is? It's not the large amount of money you've given me; it's that you have taken an interest in me; yes, Mr Tuna, that's what's precious: that you have taken an interest in *me*.

Aydın Tuna:

İnci, you talk about what's precious, but where does my value come from? The trillions that I've earned? Criticise me. It's very important for me today; I want the truth, warts and all.

İnci San:

You want me to tell you about yourself; it's not easy, but I'll try. I'll tell you whatever comes to mind. How I perceive you will come out in my words. What are you to me? A businessman beyond compare. What are you to others? That's none of my business. At the moment, I'm sad, glad, relaxed and stressed, all at the same time. I want to burst out laughing; I want to break down in sobs. Why did the doctor come here all flustered? You cancelling your appointments, telephone calls not being put through, something is going on, but I don't know what. Is there a black cloud hanging over our head? Why this generosity all of a sudden? I've always wanted what's best for here. Sometimes I hate you; sometimes I'm madly in love with you. You have set yourself up on such a pedestal that love and hate have become inseparable in my heart; they have become fused, one to the other. Wait, please don't interrupt me. Ever since my first week here, I've admired you. How many times I tried to attract your attention! I always wanted you to see me as a woman... Of course, I knew about those women you took to the big hotels. You did it more often in the past, now it's rarer... I would go mad with jealousy, without trying to make it obvious. Whenever those female spiders called you, I would get rid of them. I used to set up games so that you wouldn't be able to come together. I have a husband and children, and I love them very much. I'm faithful to them, but I would have made an exception for you. If you had asked me to come along with you, I would have run after you to the hotel with joy in my heart. Whenever you went there, you disgusted me, but when you came back, I loved you desperately. I've hidden my feelings until today. Why am I telling you all this? Why am I pouring my heart out to you like this? (*She starts to cry*)

Aydın Tuna: İnci, we're both very tired. What do you say? Shall we have a coffee? You know, your secret recipe...

İnci San: Alright, Mr Tuna, I'll bring some straight away.

(*İnci San exits*)

Aydın Tuna: (*To himself*) How could I have been so blind? How could I not have seen İnci for who she was? A veil of ambition must have been covering my eyes... If your mind cannot grasp what is going on behind that veil, then damn that mind... (*İnci San enters; she serves two cups of coffee. Aydın Tuna watches İnci's every movement attentively.*)

İnci San: I haven't finished explaining yet. I listened to your personal phonecalls from my office. I had them

47

install a parallel line; I wanted to know everything you were doing. Please, don't interrupt me. I knew the combination to your personal safe, too. The sums of money you set aside that you thought only you knew about, the money that came in from under the counter, the money that went out from under the counter, I know everything. I would open your secret safe in the evening after everyone had gone home and check the day's transactions.

Aydın Tuna:
(*Smiling merrily*) But nothing ever went missing from that safe.

İnci San:
Am I a thief? I never took as much as a single penny. My goal was to learn its mystery. If I had wanted to, I could have made off with a lot without you noticing, but I couldn't have brought myself to do something like that. My love prevented me from stealing from you and stopped me from damaging you, even in a spiritual way.

Aydın Tuna:
(*Cheerfully*) Am I really that careless? My secret safe is being monitored, and I don't even notice.

İnci San:
Ah, you businessmen! Generally, you only think of one thing. You only size up the people you work with when you're hiring them. After a while, your interest wanes. What you want, what you think, you normally don't even see it, or else you don't care. It's the balance sheet that interests you. That's the difference between the active and the passive: it's what brings joy or sadness. Are we making a profit or a loss? That's your litmus test. But anyway, let's

not 'talk about those things anymore... I'm worried sick; I've been feeling on edge for the last hour. Can you please explain why the doctor came? I know that a good secretary is one that doesn't ask too many questions. One who can take a hint... Think of my curiosity today as an exception. Why was the doctor so flustered? Why has your face been so pale for the past few days?

Aydın Tuna: It's nothing, dear. Let's not make mountains out of molehills. You know what good friends me and the doctor are.

İnci San: OK, then, Mr Tuna, I'll try to look convinced.

Aydın Tuna: Look, I'm going to say two things. I didn't know that you were listening into my personal phonecalls. I didn't suspect a thing: you got me! But I had noticed that you were opening my secret safe. I put all the money and documents in the safe in a certain order. I immediately notice the slightest change. I guess it's been happening for about twenty-seven or twenty-eight years. One day, I understood that the money had been counted and the documents rummaged through. I had a friend working for the police. I told him; we analysed the fingerprints. Your prints and those on the documents were identical. I didn't say anything to you about it; it was my way of testing you. Not even a single penny ever went missing.

İnci San: (*Upset and ashamed*) You mean you knew all this time? So why didn't you fire me on the spot?

Aydın Tuna: Why would I have fired you? It's not like you were doing it for your own personal gain. I've always been very pleased with your work. And we've been working together now for thirty years. I remember your first day here. You were trying to take everything in with your frightened eyes. You said here'd been a school for you, if so, you have been a star pupil... You picked up everything in such a short time. All the ins and outs of the companies, their secrets... Secretary is a very, very important position: the word means someone who can keep a secret.

İnci San: You've always been the model teacher for me. You've always put up with my mistakes. You've corrected my shortcomings. And, from time to time, when you got angry, it was never vulgar, rude or upsetting. I can hold you up as an example to other bosses.

Aydın Tuna: Oh, what beautiful words! Especially today, when I really need to hear sweet things. You working in the room next door always has always given me peace of mind. From now on, this work will continue with you. This little empire is now your responsibility. I can leave here with my mind at rest. And that's a great relief for me.

İnci San: But where are you going? I can't do it without you.

Aydın Tuna: Of course you can. You've worked here long enough by now to know how to run this company. It doesn't have to be very fast, just slowly but surely.

İnci San: God forbid! The place won't survive without you.

50

Aydın Tuna:	Oh, don't worry, it will: it has to.
İnci San:	But there are so many questions in my head! You didn't really think about me for years. If a businessman suddenly begins to get interested in something he hasn't paid attention to for years, it means something new is happening. I can't tell you how curious I am about why you were so surprisingly generous just now... You give me a super bonus, you find my husband a job, you inquire after my health, what's going on?
Aydın Tuna:	You've been working with me for more than a quarter of a century. Let's just say I'm making up for the years I've neglected you.
İnci San:	Mr Tuna, I'm afraid. Did the doctor break some bad news to you today? I'd be so devastated if he did.
Aydın Tuna:	No, nothing like that. İnci, now, tell me straight. What do you think about taking on bigger responsibilities or duties at the Holding?
İnci San:	What do you mean?
Aydın Tuna:	Head of the Board.
İnci San:	(*In unbelieving amazement*) Head of the Board? But... Mr Tuna... you are the Head of the Board...
Aydın Tuna:	No one can keep plodding on forever. Generations pass; new generations come.

İnci San: I can't do it without you; I can't be somewhere where you're not.

Aydın Tuna: Nonsense! You'll get used to it. It's a law of nature. Everyone concerned will be informed of your promotion tomorrow morning.

İnci San: But Mr Tuna, you'll still be my boss, won't you?

Aydın Tuna: People on the up have to learn how to stand on their own two feet. One day, you'll be alone.

İnci San: Everything is slowly starting to become clear to me. You only made this decision today. More than likely, just a few hours ago... There were some obstacles in my path that would have prevented me from working well. Being forced out of our home, my husband being unemployed... You sorted them all out in the wink of an eye. Now I can take your orders in peace, Mr Tuna. Give me a three-month trial period. If I'm not successful, you can dismiss me.

Aydın Tuna: I know you'll be successful. Oh, I was going to ask you, but for years I somehow never got round to doing it. How are your children? Where are they?

İnci San: Both of them have chosen their father's profession. The girl's twenty-one; she's going to be a civil engineer. It's her last year at university. She still lives at home. The boy is studying machine engineering in Germany; he's still got three years left.

Aydın Tuna: Having good children is a real source of wealth. Don't take it for granted. Do me a favour and have a word with mine next time they're here. As you know, their mother's addicted to poker. She doesn't have much time for them. My two boys had a hard time finishing high school. They're at university now.

İnci San: Don't you worry, Mr Tuna. I've spoken to them a few times here. There's a lot of empty posing, but when the going gets tough, they'll shape up.

Aydın Tuna: Hmm, when the going gets tough... Does the going have to get tough for the tough to get going? Do they have to taste Fortune's disfavour before they can become anything?

İnci San: Not everyone can be an Aydın Tuna!

Aydın Tuna: Not every woman can be a pearl like İnci.

İnci San: I think the first real test of my life starts from tomorrow. God help me.

Aydın Tuna: İnci, why don't you go home early today; tell your husband the good news. Tell him this too: you'll get a salary from the thirty-nine factories in the Holding structure and from two banks. Each one of them is fifty percent more than what you're on at the moment.

İnci San: I don't know what to say. Should I thank you, or should I be annoyed with you for promoting me to a position requiring so much responsibility?

Aydın Tuna: Responsibility is a pleasure for those who have the strength to handle it. You're ready for it. Still, let me give you a couple of pieces of advice. You don't need them, but anyway... I'm sure you'll forgive my chatter. Whatever you do, don't become a workaholic. Make time for your husband and children, who I know you really love. You can take this business forward, but make sure not to rush. Go with one foot on the brake; otherwise, you'll burn yourself out. You're rich if you spend the money you earn on beautiful things. Don't forget you're not only as rich as how much you earn, but also as how much you spend. Always take the weekend off. Make sure your husband does, too. Now, maybe you're wondering how far I managed to achieve these things. I'm ashamed to try to give you an answer to that. After a certain amount, wealth is only a number, and what wouldn't some of us businessmen do to make that number bigger. We don't hesitate to get our hands dirty; we enjoy giving our minds over to the devil. Why do we bother? To increase the number. If we debase ourselves to increase it, then shame on us. And there you have it, my dear colleague, my last request. If I say it's my last request, I know you'll do it. Working hours are from nine to six. Be sure not to work any longer than that. You have absolutely no reason to prove yourself. A little more, a little less, it makes no difference; in this world there are so many beautiful, new things you're only truly wealthy if you can notice them. Happy the man who can manage it. And I'll say one more thing. It's a confession: you mean the world to me. If I had been clever, I would have seen you before you got engaged, before I met my wife. Can eyes that see ever go blind? My poor eyes only opened today. You should go, İnci. Leave work early today. You won't have any time tomor-row.

İnci San:

OK, then, Mr Tuna. Thank you. I'm going home now. But what should I do on the way? Should I be jumping for joy because you've arranged a job for my husband, paid for the house, given me a big promotion and I'm going to get a big salary from it, and most importantly, because you've said such beautiful and special things, or should I cry my eyes out because of the reason behind it?

Aydın Tuna:

Jump for joy. And don't forget this: every genera-tion should be considered successful depending on what the following generation thinks of it and on the path it has opened. That is passing the torch.

İnci San:

Yes, Mr Tuna, I will always remember that too. Now, may I ask *you* a favour?

Aydın Tuna:

Of course.

İnci San:

Can I hug you and kiss you like a sister hugs her big brother?

Aydın Tuna:

(*They hug*) You should go now. (*İnci San exits cry-ing; Aydın Tuna dries his eyes with a handkerchief. To himself*) I don't have much time left. I should fly somewhere this evening. But first, I'll sit down and get these letters written. (*Sitting at the computer*) A load of buttons and lights! I somehow never managed to take the time to learn how this damned thing works. Anyway, is there a pox on pen and pa-per? (*He sits at his desk, and starts to write in a notepad; the lights go down; a short while passes; the lights come back on*) It's only taken me an hour to finish the three letters. Tomorrow morning, when İnci comes, she can give them out. Where can I go, now? Hmmm, the Scandinavian countries would be ideal. Switzerland is possible, too. If I ask our travel agent, everyone will have heard within the hour. They'd even tell the papers. It'd be lots of fuss and nonsense. This time I'll have to sort it out myself. I could call the information desk at the airport without giving my name. Now, let's see, what number's directory enquiries? I must have it somewhere... Well done, now call. Find the airport information desk. And find out which planes are going abroad from them. Choose a city and go out from there. It's that simple. (*He keeps calling directory enquiries; it's always engaged*) Well, I'd never have guessed there were so many people who wanted to find out phone numbers! (*He finally gets a reply, excitedly*) Could you give me the number of the airport information desk, please? (*He writes the number down, and dials the information desk with the same excitement*) Hello, I'd like to know which planes leave after six this evening, for Europe, Western Europe.

Voice on the phone: (*Airport Information Desk, impatiently*) Sir, which city would you like to go to and on which day?

Aydın Tuna: I want to go today, but I haven't decided which city, yet.

Voice on the phone: Decide, and then please call back, thank you.

Aydın Tuna:	Now look here, sweetheart, is it really that difficult to list the planes that take off from the airport after six o'clock?
Voice on the phone:	No, you listen to me! I'm not your sweetheart. I take no pleasure from this fake intimacy. I'm just some ugly girl on the other end of the phone. Do you have the time? Do you want me to describe myself to you?
Aydın Tuna:	(*As if he is enjoying the conversation*) Oh, please do!
Voice on the phone:	Two bulging, dark grey eyes... Sunken cheeks... A big mouth and two buck teeth... A Roman nose... There are hairs like a moustache between my mouth and nose. I have to have it waxed. Moving on to my body, I was last in the queue when they were handing out anything you could call aesthetic. Small tits, big bum... If you saw me, you wouldn't be able to think of anything to say to console me.
Aydın Tuna:	Come on, you're not being serious!
Voice on the phone:	That's up to you to decide. Anyway, why don't you go to a travel agent? Tell them what you want. They'll let you know what times you can fly and the cheapest price.
Aydın Tuna:	I don't want to phone a travel agency. And a cheap price isn't important.
Voice on the phone:	And a visa? Turkish citizens cannot set foot outside the country without a visa. But, of course, that's

none of my business.

Aydın Tuna: In that case, just do what's in your job description.

Voice on the phone: That's all well and good, but you're not acting normally. You're asking about planes that will leave the country in three hours. What if you've killed someone, or if you want to flee the country? It wouldn't be right for me to pass on information to a murderer. Why would anyone just suddenly up and leave for a different country?

Aydın Tuna: (*Amused*) I haven't killed anyone.

Voice on the phone: Or else your a conman... Gathering a fortune, and then heading for the hills... Catch as catch can.

Aydın Tuna: (*Cheerfully*) You can be sure; I haven't swindled anybody.

Voice on the phone: You're not one of the writer-artist set, are you? You've put pen to paper and hit on something taboo. Someone takes offence. Prison, this, that... Are you forbidden to leave the country?

Aydın Tuna: No, I'm not. You have to believe me.

Voice on the phone: I know. You're not a killer or a conman or forbidden to leave the country.

Aydın Tuna: (*As if he wants to draw out the conversation*) How do you know? Maybe I'm lying. What if I am one of them?

Voice on the phone:	You're not. It's obvious from the modulations of your voice that you're not lying...
Aydın Tuna:	From the modulations? What's that? You work out if someone's telling the truth or not from the modulations of their voice?
Voice on the phone:	Of course. Look, just like fingerprints, voice modulations change from person to person. The modulations, the increases and decreases in volume of the voice, give you away. I immediately understand if what you're saying is true or not.
Aydın Tuna:	Like a lie detector?
Voice on the phone:	Yes, that's right.
Aydın Tuna:	Well how does it work?
Voice on the phone:	It's not something you can learn from a book; there are no rules. Let's say it's an extra sense. Let's say it's the seventh sense, or maybe the tenth. Some people have it from birth. For example, good businessmen... Politicians can have it, too.
Aydın Tuna:	Why don't you use this talent in other areas? For example, in a big company or in the Foreign Office.
Voice on the phone:	Do you think it's that easy to find a job? Where can you find one if you don't have contacts? The Foreign Office is a dream – forget about it. Or a big company, well, if you don't know someone on the inside, then that's just another dream.

Aydın Tuna:	Have you ever applied? Maybe someone will hire you.
Voice on the phone:	Companies put ads in the papers. Columns and columns of oversized ads... And you apply. For nothing! Some of them don't even write back. But in the end, they hire someone. Nepotism... Shall I tell you what they say in America? "It's not what you know, it's who you know." You need to have someone behind you until you get a job. Once you've got a job, rising up the ladder might be linked to your ability. But sometimes ability is of no importance.
Aydın Tuna:	For example?
Voice on the phone:	You could sleep your way to the top...
Aydın Tuna:	OK, I see what you're saying. Anyway, can you tell me which big companies you've applied to? I'm curious.
Voice on the phone:	Gök Holding, Demir Holding, Tuna Holding, and there was another one, what was it now? I can't remember at the moment. You apply to their HR department. And you're left banging your head against a brick wall; you don't get a peep from the other side.
Aydın Tuna:	I'm going to speak to you pleasantly for a few minutes. It's clear that you're an intelligent person. Can you give me your name, please?
Voice on the phone:	It's Ayşe Nur. Please don't tell anyone that I was gossiping to you on the job. It's against the rules. I

could get fired for it. You notice how I'm not asking you who you are. You wouldn't tell me anyway.

Aydın Tuna: What kind of a person am I? Tell me according to the modulations of my voice, using your seventh or tenth sense. Can you do that?

Voice on the phone: I'll have a go. You're a man of the world, experienced, completely sure of yourself, quite contrary, quick to fly off the handle, used to always giving orders... I think you're someone who has been a little spoiled by the adulation of those around you. You could be a doctor or a lecturer. Maybe you're a powerful businessman; that's possible, too.

Aydın Tuna: A businessman? Now, where did you get that from?

Voice on the phone: There's a strong chance you are. As soon as you picked up the phone, you perceived me like a member of staff who works with you. Typical businessman behaviour. You saying "sweetheart" was really just a kind of camouflage. You're actually thinking of hiding what's going on.

Aydın Tuna: What am I camouflaging? What am I hiding?

Voice on the phone: "Hey, parasite employee, answer my questions immediately. And don't poke your nose into things that are not part of your job." That's what you meant to say.

Aydın Tuna: No, you're exaggerating. Anyway, what else do the modulations of my voice whisper to you?

Voice on the phone: You're someone who is approaching something better, more perfect, step by step. It's something you've been instilling in yourself. It's a conscious way of handling the fear in your unconscious.

Aydın Tuna: It's not easy to follow what you say, but still, thank you.

Voice on the phone: Let me tell you the international flights after six: Paris, London, Moscow, Milan, Amsterdam...

Aydın Tuna: (*Interrupting her*) That's enough, thank you. It's been a pleasure talking to you.

Voice on the phone: It's been a one-sided getting to know you. You know my name, but I don't know yours. Before hanging up, I should apologise for my insolence a few moments ago. I don't know what psychological reason you had, but thank you for calling me sweetheart. It must be a great honour to be your girlfriend. It must have been a subtle compliment for you to say that. And one more thing... I'm not ugly, either; I'm twenty-four, and my fiancé keeps telling me that I'm very beautiful.

Aydın Tuna: I'm sure that you are beautiful.

Voice on the phone: Have a nice day, whoever you are. And have a nice trip wherever you're going.

Aydın Tuna: Thank you, thank you very much. (*He hangs up. He looks around for a short while and says to himself*) I don't have much time. The best thing would be to go to London first and carry on from there. If

I take my small bag with me, that should be enough. (*Stopping as if he has just remembered something*) I'll recommend that girl at the information desk to İnci. She'd make a good secretary. (*He picks up the dictaphone*) İnci, you were looking for a secretary. There's a girl who applied to us in writing. She's called Ayşe Nur. She works at the information desk at the airport. I spoke to her, but I didn't tell her who I was. Take a look at her application. (*He puts the dictaphone down; his eye dwells on the medicine cabinet on the wall*) It's time for me to stop using them. (*Shouting*) Drugs, you don't help me to live, so I can die without any help from you too. Your road leads to hell. You don't have the strength to make my illness go away. Damn the lot of you. (*He opens the door of the medicine cabinet and empties it out into the wastepaper basket. He goes as far as the door with a small travelling bag in his hand and then turns to look at his desk*) Dear office, now it's time for me to say good bye to you. Of course, sadness is part of saying good bye but not in how I'm saying it. I've got used to it. I'm a businessman whose days are numbered and whose liver's wracked with cancer. So, what's to be done? I've had many good days here. My good days will continue in my little palace six feet under. The main thing is I'm looking for somewhere where there's no trickery or ambition. I know that there isn't really anywhere like that. I'm going to form a place, a point like that in my brain, and then I'll look at the heaven I've created and pat myself on the back. That's what I'll do. I'm flying this evening to a London that I've been two at least a hundred times but which I've never seen. I'll shake the very dust out of the city. I'll wander its streets for hours. Museums, theatres, musicals, cinemas, this and that, whatever there is to see, I'm going to go down the whole list. Forty years ago, when I first went, I saw a place called "Speakers' Corner." In the corner of a huge park, groups of people listen to speakers. Anyone can say whatever they want: there are no limits. Whoever wants to give a speech, can come and have a go. Say whatever comes to your lips or your mind. Some will clap; some will boo. That day, there was a bald man praising all religions and saying we were all brothers. Thirty metres along, a black man with thick hair and thin as a rake was shouting that MPs shouldn't be paid a wage, that they made more than enough on bribes. In a different place, a girl in a miniskirt was defending the thesis that prostitutes be paid a salary by the state. I'll go to that park tomorrow. What was it called? Ah yes, Hyde Park... Let's say that I'm a speaker there and that I'm giving a speech to anyone who'll listen. "Ladies and Gentlemen! Let me paint a picture for you. It's called the picture of life. On the left of the picture, let there be enough food and drink to give you pleasure, but not enough to harm you. Let's say you have enough money and property for a comfortable life, but nothing to get too excited over. On the right of the picture, let there be paintings, sculpture and fine arts. Something else! Let there be literature with its poetry, stories and plays. And something else, let there be music with its songs and instruments. If you don't have these, or if you don't have enough of them, you don't have that life, or, at least, not enough of it. (*Looking towards*

the audience) You, with the goatee beard, what are
you yelling about? I'm the one who's talking nonsense, am I? I think like that because I'm poor, do
I? Why on earth do you think I'm poor? From my
clothes? What's wrong with my clothes? A cotton
shirt and linen trousers. Well, what kind of clothes
do the wealthy wear? I mean, should I have come
here in a dinner jacket? Can't the rich come to this
park, then? Well, why the hell not? The rich work
hard to make themselves richer, and when they
have the time, they go places where other rich
people can see them. Who are you saying comes
here the most? Communists, atheists, religious
fundamentalists, gays, lesbians and penniless intel-
lectuals... You're wrong, my friend. This park is
open to everyone who wants to explain his ideas.
I'm the utopian dreamer, am I? Look, you've started
to get on my nerves. I don't speak this much with
everyone, you know. And now you're asking me
which country I'm from and what my religion is!
Why don't you just mind your own business! Think
about what I've said. Is it right or wrong? That's
the important thing. You wonder if I'm a Christian.
I'm not. And I'm not a Jew. And I'm not a Muslim.
And I'm not a Buddhist, and I'm not an atheist. So
what am I? I'm all of them and none of them.
What's my nationality? There are about one hundred and fifty countries in the world, and I walk
around with about one hundred and fifty passports.
What did you say? What did you say? I'm just a
hard-up madman, am I? I'm not, and I can't get
angry with you for those insults. I'm making fun of
you, you say? Definitely not. Why don't I belong to
any religion or nationality? At any rate, won't God,

who we call that greatest power, embrace us all one day and hold us in his strong arms? Everyone is naked and equal there. If you believe that, then you'll understand me. Listen to what I'm going to suggest to you. Imagine the picture I painted for you a short while ago, and look for yourself there. If you are lacking in some aspects, try to acquire them. Do what you can with a good intent. If you say it doesn't matter, you're nothing. Do you understand now? Good bye... Oh, were you going to say something? I'm listening. You're right: being rich, or, as you say, a "comprador", shouldn't be considered the most important element of life. I put property and money on the left of the picture I painted, but I placed the visual arts, literature and music on the right. Now, please listen to me well. Generally, the poets, the writer/artist set, musicians and the great masters of the visual arts disdain money and possessions, or at least try to make it look as if they do. Just like those who say that money and possessions are not very important to them. They tend to look down on businessmen. And because businessmen can feel this, they look down on people who claim to be artists. This mutual looking down on each other and, at the same time, this envy, that's where the seeds of misunderstanding are to be found. Now tell me, my friend, what's the difference between opening a factory and doing something artistic? Both need self-sacrifice; both are products of experience. Both bear the ideal of bringing society to a better place. And there is infinite pleasure and satisfaction in this ideal. If only artists and factory owners could come together more frequently, and if only they could win people's hearts and minds, together. What do you say now? Am I still a utopian dreamer? Clap or boo, but whatever you do, my goateed friend, good bye." (*Taking a deep breath*) Well, dear office of mine, what do you think about me making a speech like that tomorrow in Hyde Park? After London, I'll travel a little around England and then Scotland. From there to Paris... (*He sings a Parisian song*) From Paris to the Black Forest... (*He hums Lili Marleen*) Then, Vienna, give me your hand. (*He sings one of Strauss' waltzes and dances along to it*) Then comes the turn of Fatma the Easel's great love, Italy. Rome, Florence, Venice and Sicily... (*He sings La Donna è mobile, and stops a moment*) Open your arms, Spain, and welcome me... (*He hums a Spanish song*) and Lisbon... (*He sings Adieu Lisbon*) and then, my friends, the play is over; the curtain shall fall. (*He stops for a moment; the funeral march begins to play from the loudspeaker. Aydın Tuna goes to the end of the stage, puts his right hand on his heart, and walks slowly with his back to the audience, keeping time to the music; the stage lights go down for a short while... The music stops; the lights come back on. Looking at his desk*) Do you know who I really feel sorry for? For the one who'll work at this desk from now on. Take good care of your new boss. Bye now. (*He exits, a small travel bag in his hand, his head held high*)

Scene Four

Another office: İnci San's office. İnci San is wearing a chic but plain dress. In the office, there are also two young men, twenty and twenty-three years old. They are wearing jeans and colourful t-shirts. They are Aydın Tuna's sons. The younger one is chewing gum. The older one is looking around blankly.

İnci San:

In these three letters, your father has written that he set off on a journey yesterday. One of the letters is for you, one for your mother, and the third one, for the staff. The three letters were all left open, not put in envelopes. He wants me to hand them out. (*She holds up a note*) I think you'll want to know what your father has written to you. (*The letter can be read out over the loudspeaker in Aydın Tuna's voice, or, if desired, one of the sons can read it out*)

To My Dear Sons, Erhan and Çelik,

Today, I'm setting out on what you could call a long journey. I don't imagine you'll be too put out by the fact that I couldn't find the time to say good bye.

As your father, I know that it is necessary for me to say a few things. I don't want to give you advice. It's not necessary, and anyway experience is the best teacher.

The intelligent person is someone who can learn from others' experiences, especially from their successes and mistakes. Anyone who doesn't or can't do this is possessed of a brain with only a limited field of perception.

You both really like driving. It's natural at your age. Don't be sad if you have an accident while under the influence. If you end up in hospital, the doctors will save you; if you end up in a police station, your mother will save you, giving my name, of course. What can be said if there's nothing the doctors can do? You make your own bed, so you have to lie on it.

You don't have to work, either. As it is, in the company and the factories I have founded, there are thousands of people producing things using their mental or physical effort. You are, by a stroke of chance, partners in this production. It's just that, if one day the workers don't want to give you even a sniff of their mental and physical products, then you'll put your heads in your hands and start to think. And that wouldn't be such a bad thing. Starting to think is a positive thing. Some people even enjoy it.

By the authority invested in me by the Board, I have promoted Mrs San to CEO. From now on, she is your boss. If you choose to work, I'm sure she will be able to assist you, but if you find that idleness suits your swagger better, I only have one thing to say to you: I wash my hands of you.

Love and kisses,
Dad

Çelik Tuna: And that's supposed to be a letter?

Erhan Tuna: It's not a letter: it's a proclamation.

Çelik Tuna:	Up sticks, go on a journey without telling anyone, don't even bother to phone your sons... Have we really sunk that low in his eyes?
Erhan Tuna:	Mrs San, where has our dad gone, and how long will he be away for? You of all people must know.
İnci San:	He didn't tell me, either.
Çelik Tuna:	Well, that's a bit strange, isn't it? Are we supposed to believe that? You're the number one person in our companies now, and dad just upped and left without telling you a thing. Is that what you're trying to say?
İnci San:	Read the letter well a few times over. All the answers are hidden there, for those who can find them, of course.
Erhan Tuna:	Çelik, mate, it's not just the English that God hates: look, he's sent us our very own Iron Lady, too.
Çelik Tuna:	Erhan, mate, it's a little empire here. You and me, we're just citizens. It doesn't have to give us information about internal and external affairs. Have you got that? It's that simple. (*The telephone rings*)
Voice on the phone:	(*The switchboard*) Mrs San, it's your representative; he's phoning from Japan.
İnci San:	Put him through to the office next door. (*Looking sternly at Aydın Tuna's sons*) Wait here; I've got some things to say to you. (*She exits*)

Erhan Tuna:	Ooh, now we've made the Iron Lady angry, and dad isn't here. Everything's in that woman's hands. You saw what the letter said. Your boss is İnci San. If you choose to work, I'm sure she will be able to assist you; if you don't, I wash my hands of you. What's that supposed to mean, then?
Çelik Tuna:	It means when the shit hits the fan, it's none of his business.
Erhan Tuna:	So what are we going to do now?
Çelik Tuna:	What did we learn when we were doing our National Service? We're going to do a recce! In critical positions, current strength can be measured and adapted. You begin...
Erhan Tuna:	This is a huge holding company. Who's in charge at the moment? İnci San a.k.a. the Iron Lady... Dad's right-hand God only knows what... It's not clear where dad is, or at least, the Iron Lady and the Doctor know, but they're hiding it from us. Who are we? Two zeros... We've got nothing to do with anything.
Çelik Tuna:	Why don't we ask the Doctor?
Erhan Tuna:	He's such a mason; he'd rather die than tell us anything. There's no point in even asking...
Çelik Tuna:	There'd better not be a woman involved in all of this.

Erhan Tuna:	I don't think there is. Why would he suddenly disappear because of a woman? He wouldn't do something like that.
Çelik Tuna:	Where was the Iron Lady's son studying? Germany, wasn't it? And she's got a daughter at university, too. If she brings them here one day, she'll have a full crew. She'll tell us to fuck off. Has that sunk in? There's nothing we can do about it. The Iron Lady, her son and her daughter will be running the place, and we'll be left empty-handed.
Erhan Tuna:	Exactly. And this is a joint stock company. Here's my idea: didn't dad tell us to work? Well, let's do that. Let's advance the Tuna name in this holding. Let's show everyone that we're Aydın Tuna's sons. Come on, Çelik, lets show them what we're made off. (*The telephone rings*)
Voice on the phone:	(*The switchboard*) Çelik Tuna, a friend of yours is calling. It's Adnan.
Erhan Tuna:	I'm not Çelik; I'm Erhan. But it doesn't really make a difference. Put him through.
Voice on the phone:	(*Adnan*) Çelik, mate, I want my reward, OK? We're going to Bodrum. Not tomorrow, but the day after... The chicks have been sorted. Real babes. If they're walking down the street, you can be sure that any man who doesn't look after them and sigh is queer. We're going the day after tomorrow, OK, mate?
Erhan Tuna:	Adnan, I'm Erhan. And I gotta tell you I can't make

it. Wait a mo, I'll give you Çelik.

Voice on the phone:	Hey, why can't you come?
Çelik Tuna:	Adnan, I'm Çelik. Look, Adnan, mate, I'm not coming, either. I'm really sorry, but there's really no way I can.
Voice on the phone:	What's wrong? What's the problem?
Çelik Tuna:	Dad gave us something to do. We've got to stay here and do it.
Voice on the phone:	God! We're only going to be away for four days. Your dad has never given you anything to do before. What's happened all of a sudden? It's just four little days.
Çelik Tuna:	Impossible, we've got to stay here. We can't come.
Voice on the phone:	Give me Erhan.
Erhan Tuna:	Adnan, mate, look, I'll give you the low down. Dad gave me and Çelik something to do. We have to do it. (*Stressing each word*) **We can't come.**
Voice on the phone:	For God's sake what kind of mission are you on that you can't postpone it for four measly days.
Erhan Tuna:	Look here, if Aydın Tuna gives you something to do, it has to be done. It can't be delayed, canceled, postponed or protested. You understand? That job has to be done. Don't think he gives us special treatment just because he's our dad.

Voice on the phone: But I've already arranged the girls and the hotel; I've paid the hotel for three double rooms for a four-night stay. Mr Tuna likes me. I'll have a word with him. He'll give you four days off. I'll ask him really nicely.

Erhan Tuna: That's impossible because he's gone on a trip.

Voice on the phone: Where's he gone?

Erhan Tuna: I don't know.

Voice on the phone: Mate, you've gone crazy all of a sudden. Your dad's gone on a trip, and you say you don't know where he's gone. I'm not a bloody journalist. Why are you keeping it from me? Wait, let me tell you. He's gone to Japan, hasn't he? To make an agreement with the electronics industry. I read it in the paper two days ago.

Erhan Tuna: Could be, maybe he has gone to Japan.

Voice on the phone: Stop playing with my head! What does could be mean. We're mates, aren't we? I mean, look, I've invested all my money in your holding's shares. If there's something bad, tell me, or else I'm shafted.

Erhan Tuna: Don't worry; there's nothing bad. I'm serious about Bodrum, though. It's just not doable. We'll pay the hotel money when we come. And what do you say about taking those two girls out to dinner on Sunday evening?

Voice on the phone: OK, then, mate. I'll do my best, my utmost. But if the Holding's situation goes tits up, let me know.

Erhan Tuna: Don't worry. Everything's fine: we're in charge. You don't have to fear the worst. (*He hangs up*)

Çelik Tuna: First, let's go home and get changed. This is the nerve centre of a Holding, not a stadium.

Erhan Tuna: The Iron Lady said to wait here. If she doesn't see us here when she comes back, she'll get angry.

Çelik Tuna: Let's leave a message with her secretary, saying we've gone to get changed, and we'll be back in an hour. Come on, let's get a move on. (*They exit. The stage lights go out; a short while goes by; the lights are on again; Çelik Tuna and Erhan Tuna are dressed very smartly. İnci San enters; on seeing her, both of them rise to their feet and wait respectfully*)

İnci San: Oh, you're back, then. Very chic... It must be a lot of fun to work with young men this handsome. I'll ask you this first. Have you seen the letter your father wrote to the employees of the holding company? (*Getting no for an answer*) Well, read it now then.

Dear Valued Employees of the Companies attached to Tuna Holding,

I am leaving on a long journey. I cannot give you more detailed information on this subject, but rest assured that I will not take too much of your time.

I would like to thank each and every one of you individually. Your knowledge and your experience

have been invaluable; in short, had it not been for your mental and physical contributions, we would never have been able to rise to the level at which we find ourselves today. Thank you.

We can succeed in anything, whatever it might be, with the joint efforts of all of the employees. Your holding has made it a point of honour to evaluate this effort and reward you for it in the fairest way possible. This is a principle that we underestimate at our peril.

In addition to this, I request the relevant colleagues to distribute ten percent of pre-tax profits to company employees according to their band on the pay scale, on an annual basis.

In accordance with the powers invested in me by the Holding's Board of Directors, I have promoted my personal assistant, Mrs İnci San, to Head the Board of Directors of the Holding and the companies linked to the Holding. Mrs İnci San is a colleague who, for the past thirty years, has, by means of her professional approach and her natural skills, been able to put her signature to our growth. I congratulate her on her new appointment.

Valued managers and employees, I salute you with respect and brotherly love.

Signed
Aydın Tuna

Çelik Tuna: Well, I'll be... If it wasn't for his handwriting, I would have sworn it wasn't written by dad.

Erhan Tuna: Look, all the workers have become dad's brothers with one stroke of the pen.

Çelik Tuna: Let's work out how many uncles we've got now. (*Turning to İnci San, with respect*) Mrs San, do you approve of our dad's decision? I mean this thing about ten percent...

İnci San: I've been here for more than a quarter of a century. In his professional life, I have never seen your father take a wrong decision. Otherwise, how could he have become the owner of thirty-nine companies and two banks? Let me say it again, in his professional life, whatever your father did, he did it at the right time and place. Now, let's go to my office and draw up a work plan for you two. (*They exit; the lights go down*)

(*The same office; it is empty. The telephone rings*)

Over the loudspeaker: (*A man's voice, Ahmet Ok*) Could I speak to Ayşe Nur, please.

Over the loudspeaker: (*A woman's voice, Ayşe Nur*) Speaking.

Over the loudspeaker: This is Tuna Holding's HR department; I'm Ahmet Ok.

Over the loudspeaker: Hello, Mr Ok.

Over the loudspeaker: You have applied to us for a job as a secretary. We have looked at your application form. You will have a three-month probation period. We accept the desired salary you wrote on your form. When can you start?

Over the loudspeaker: Would the beginning of next month be suitable, Mr Ok?

Over the loudspeaker: If I were you, I would go for the beginning of next week.

Over the loudspeaker: Of course, that's fine. I'll start on Monday morning, then.

Over the loudspeaker: Come to our department in the holding building on Monday morning at nine o'clock. I will take you to Mrs San.

Over the loudspeaker: Who is Mrs San?

Over the loudspeaker: Mrs San is head of the Tuna Holding's Board of Directors.

Over the loudspeaker: Isn't Mr Tuna the Head of the Board?

Over the loudspeaker: He was... Until yesterday... Yesterday, sometime in the mid-afternoon, Mr Tuna handed over the Headship of the Board of Directors to Mrs San. He has gone on a trip.

Over the loudspeaker: Thank you very much. I look forward to meeting you on Monday morning.

Over the loudspeaker: Bye, then. (*He hangs up*)

Over the loudspeaker: (*Excitedly*) Oh my God, so it *was* him: that voice on the phone yesterday evening was his voice. I've spoken to Aydın Tuna. It was definitely him. He hadn't decided where he was going to go. But why? Why?

---END OF ACT ONE---

ACT TWO – Scene One

A small town in Sicily. Aydın Tuna gets out of an intercity minibus. He looks around cheerfully. A 16–18 year-old comes up to him. It is Vittorio. He is wearing a t-shirt and linen trousers. Aydın Tuna is similarly dressed.

Vittorio:	Buon Giorno.
Aydın Tuna:	Good morning.
Vittorio:	I can speak English, too. Are you looking for some-one or somewhere, Sir? Can I help you? I have the time, and the thing that sets this region apart is that we are all kind and welcoming.
Aydın Tuna:	(*Looking the young man up and down carefully*) Thank you, kind and welcoming Sicilian. I'm looking for a hotel.
Vittorio:	A hotel? The expert is standing in front of you, Sir. What kind of hotel? Cheap or expensive? How many stars? I don't recommend going to one with too many, Sir. They're all the same. Once you've stayed in one, you've stayed in them all.
Aydın Tuna:	I want a hotel that isn't too noisy, but comfortable, clean and near the sea. Oh, and the food must be delicious.
Vittorio:	It's clear to see that you are a gentleman of re-fined taste, Sir. I'll recommend you a guesthouse. You will close your eyes and say that you are in heaven. Heaven, I tell you. It's very close to the

sea. The rooms are neither too big nor too small. The food is not the mass-produced stuff you get at hotels with lots of stars. It's like the food a mother makes for her well-loved children, singing songs of joy. It's finger-licking good, I tell you.

Aydın Tuna:	Is it your guesthouse or a relative's?
Vittorio:	How did you guess? I give up!
Aydın Tuna:	It was the way you told it, my Sicilian friend. You can only be talking about your own house with your voice trembling with pride and your eyes sparkling with joy. Only your own. What's your name?
Vittorio:	Vittorio Giorgio, Sir. The name of our guesthouse is Guesthouse Luigia. Luigia is my big sister, Sir. And may I ask you something, Sir? What's your name? You speak English very well, but it's clear to see you're not English.
Aydın Tuna:	Well, I'm Aydın Tuna; I'm Turkish, from Istanbul.
Vittorio:	I couldn't study very much, Sir. For personal reasons... But didn't they used to call it Constantinople, Sir?
Aydın Tuna:	Yes, it did use to be called Constantinople. But the Turks captured the city in 1453 and changed its name to Istanbul.
Vittorio:	They say Istanbul is even more beautiful than Sicily. Is that true?

Aydın Tuna:	Well, it's only my first day here! After I've had a good wander round everywhere, I'll tell you which one is more beautiful.
Vittorio:	(*Reluctantly*) There's something I should tell you, Sir. Our guesthouse is two hundred Euro a night, and you have to pay three days in advance. That's not too much, Sir, is it?
Aydın Tuna:	Maybe not. It's a deal. I'll pay up front now. Here you are, six hundred Euro for three nights... (*Turning to the audience*) The cheek of it! When he heard I was Turkish, he thought I was going to haggle with him. He asked for at least three times the going rate! But anyway, he seems like a good lad, I suppose. (*He turns to Vittorio*) I'll make all the other payments after this one by credit card.
Vittorio :	(*Takes the money as if he is going to jump for joy*) Of course, Sir, however you wish. Now, please, hop in the old banger. The gates of heaven have opened: angels await us. May I ask a favour of you? We'll be passing by a bank soon. I'm going to pay five hundred Euro of the money you gave me into the bank. Could you wait in the car for a few minutes?
Aydın Tuna:	Of course, go ahead, it's no problem at all . Are you afraid of carrying so much money around with you?
Vittorio:	No, Signor Tuna, it's not that. We've mortgaged our house, you see, I mean, our guesthouse. Every month, we have to pay at least five hundred Euro. I'll pay in what you've just given me.

81

Aydın Tuna:	A mortgage? But why?
Vittorio:	My sister can tell you better than I can. Which one would you prefer: for my sister to tell you, or for me to?
Aydın Tuna:	Well, you can begin and your sister can fill in the blanks. It'll give us something to talk about on the way, what do you say?
Vittorio:	That would be good, Sir. Well, here we are in front of the bank. I'll be back in around fifteen minutes, Sir. (*He runs out of the car; Aydın Tuna closes his eyes and waits; Vittorio comes running back to the car*)
Aydın Tuna:	Have you paid it in?
Vittorio:	Of course, here's the receipt; I'm going to give it to my sister. (*He gives the receipt to Aydın Tuna, who takes off his glasses and examines it carefully; he gives it back to Vittorio*)
Aydın Tuna:	Now, let's hear what you've got to say. Why did ycu mortgage your house? Give me all the details... There's no hurry.
Vittorio:	Ten years ago, we had a minimarket. My mum, my dad, my sister and me, we were a very happy family. I was still at primary school then. Then, my father caught the bad disease. My mum and my sister looked after him very well, but things took a turn for the worse. My dad was bedridden. It was difficult to run the minimarket. It's not a job for

two women after all, is it, Sir?

Aydın Tuna:	No, I don't think it is. Anyway, go on.
Vittorio:	My dad hired someone to take care of the mini-market, but, unfortunately, he turned out to be a thief. Of course, we didn't know he was going to be a rotten apple. The minimarket started tc lose money right, left and centre.
Aydın Tuna:	So what did your father do to try and stop it?
Vittorio:	At around the same time, he got a Sicilian to ask for my sister's hand. He was a strange man. He came to the house a few times. They said he was very rich. My dad's illness got worse and worse. My mum and dad wanted my sister to marry that Sicilian, so the family would have been saved.
Aydın Tuna:	Well, did your sister want to marry him?
Vittorio:	No, Sir, she didn't. She didn't think he was right for her. Even the neighbours were trying to persuade her. We were in debt and we had no idea how we were going to pay it off.
Aydın Tuna:	How come you were in debt?
Vittorio:	The man who we got to work for us in the mini-market was under-recording sales and pocketing the difference. Purchases were recorded as debts. We were in such a bad way what with my dad seriously ill, my mum not knowing what to do and up to our necks in debt that in the end, my sister

caved in and married him.

Aydın Tuna: And what happened next?

Vittorio: The man who'd told us he was rich turned out to be lacking, not only in money, but also in moral fibre. He fired the man from the minimarket and somehow got him to pay back the money he had stolen, but we didn't see a penny of it. He spent all of it on gambling and women. He passed the minimarket's debts on to my sister with his dirty tricks.

Aydın Tuna: And how did he behave towards your sister?

Vittorio: Very badly... He sometimes even used to hit her. He slapped her three times in front of me. He would get into debt and get my sister to sign the certificates. If she refused, he would beat her mercilessly. I used to get really upset and start to cry.

Aydın Tuna: I think that's normal; it's not easy to be able to cope with all that. Anyway, what happened after that?

Vittorio: Mum and dad understood that they'd made a mistake. Dad slowly withered away and died. He died some time after my sister's wedding. My mum was devasted, and five months after that we lost her too to a heart attack.

Aydın Tuna: It's very painful for both teller and listener. What was wrong with your father?

Vittorio: It was cancer, Sir. They said that he didn't stand a

---

chance anyway. My dad was a very good person. He never stole a single penny from anyone. But still, I don't think he's gone to heaven.

Aydın Tuna: Why not, if he was so good? If he wasn't a thief?

Vittorio: They forced my sister to get married. When we went to the church, her eyes were all puffy from crying. My sister says it would be wrong for mum and dad to be sent to heaven because they ruined her life for their own interests. There was no need for that marriage. The minimarket was sold; the guesthouse was sold; the debts were paid back. There was nothing they could do for my dad anyway.

Aydın Tuna: Well, what are things like now? What does your brother-in-law, your sister's husband, do?

Vittorio: Ah, we've got to the best bit. The bastard was killed. He had links with the Mafia. They say that he wanted to be a godfather. Someone shot him, but we don't know who. One Sunday, after he had beaten my sister for no apparent reason, he left the house and went to church to pray. When he left the church, he passed by the town square. As he was walking past, his hands behind his back like the local hard man, he was shot. The bullet entered his back. "Where's that fucker?" he bellowed. A second bullet hit him in the hip. A third, his shoulder... He gave up the ghost crawling along the ground. Nobody wanted to take him in their car and get him to hospital.

Aydın Tuna:	Well, they do say that the pitcher that goes often to the well comes home broken at last. I suppose your sister wasn't particularly upset by her husband's death?
Vittorio:	We celebrated. She drank champagne; I was young, so I drank grape juice. The day my brother-in-law was killed, my sister started looking ten or maybe fifteen years younger.
Aydın Tuna:	Do you have any nephews or nieces?
Vittorio:	Luckily, they didn't have any children. I don't think it's right for a woman to have children by someone she hates. I think my sister was on the pill. Maybe it's wrong of me to say something like that to you? At least, I hope you don't think I'm too talkative.
Aydın Tuna:	Not at all. So anyway when your brother-in-law was killed, you sold the minimarket to cover your debts, and when that wasn't enough, you mortgaged the guesthouse.
Vittorio:	Yes, Sir, that's exactly how it was.
Aydın Tuna:	Now, if you don't mind, I think I'll take a short nap. I'm so tired. But, please, don't drive too fast.
Vittorio:	I won't go any faster than a tortoise. (*A while passes*) Signor Tuna, we're here, Sir. Our little heaven is here.

(*The hall of a house that has been turned into a guesthouse. The back of the house is a garden. At the front, there is a small path leading to the sea.*

A woman's voice singing a Neapolitan song can be heard. Vittorio and Aydın Tuna enter. A pretty, thirty to thirty-five year old woman meets them)

Vittorio: Let me introduce you: Mr Aydın Tuna, Luigia Gior-
                   gio.

Luigia: Welcome, Signor Tuna.

Vittorio: Luigia, this is our first Turkish guest. He's from Is-
                   tanbul.

Luigia: That's wonderful. Yes, our first Turkish guest. When
                   you say Istanbul, it makes me dream... I'm going
                   over the deep blue clouds on a flying carpet and
                   gliding onto the bridge that joins Asia and Europe. Is-
                   tanbul is a really unique city, isn't it, Signor Tuna?

Aydın Tuna: Yes, it definitely is. Mrs Giorgio, you should come
                   as soon as you have the chance and make your dream
                   come true. What do you say?

Luigia: It's difficult, but why not? (*To Vittorio*) Vittorio, can
                   you show Signor Tuna his room? (*To Aydın Tuna*)
                   Signor Tuna, could I have your passport, please? I
                   have to take down your details. (*She takes his pass-
                   port. Aydın Tuna and Vittorio exit. Luigia, to herself*)
                   What a nice man. His face is pale, but he looks
                   healthy. (*She examines his passport*) Sixty-five years
                   old. What a fine fellow, though. All these visas and
                   stamps, the man has travelled the world. If I'd trav-
                   elled that much, I suppose I'd get tired, too.

(*Vittorio enters*)

87

Vittorio:	He likes the room.
Luigia:	How long is he going to stay? Did you ask him?
Vittorio:	Three days, I mean three nights. Now, listen to what I have to say. You'll be over the moon.
Luigia:	(*Worried*) I hope you haven't put your foot in it. Sometimes you're like a bull in a china shop...
Vittorio:	Why won't you trust me? Do you know what I've done? I got six hundred Euro off that Turk.
Luigia:	Six hundred Euro? For what?
Vittorio:	What do you think it's for? A three-night stay...
Luigia:	(*Gasping*) Just wait, you took six hundred Euro for three nights?
Vittorio:	Yeah, you see how talented I am. Six hundred Euro for three nights... And you say I'm no good for anything...
Luigia:	(*Still in shock*) You mean to say that you asked for six hundred Euro and he immediately got it out and gave it to you? Well, where's the money then?
Vittorio:	Well, seeing we've got our mortgage repayments, I paid five hundred of it into the bank. Here's the receipt. (*With gravity*) Now do you see how clever your brother is?

Luigia: It's unbelievable. You asked for six hundred Euro, and he didn't object, and, without even seeing the place, he handed the money over to you.

Vittorio: My expertise played a big role in it, I tell you. I praised the guesthouse. I was very convincing. I explained the difference between us and a five-star hotel lyrically.

Luigia: Tell me something. It's fifty Euro a night here. Why did you ask for two hundred?

Vittorio: You remember I went to that Hotel and Tourism course. Our teacher told us that Turks and Yugoslavs haggle a lot. But this Aydın Tuna didn't object at all. He said OK.

Luigia: (*Shouting*) Oh, my stupid brother! What do you think you're doing quadrupling the price? What if he finds out the real price or complains? They'll close us down! Do you think conning people is something to be proud of?

Vittorio: (*Obstinately*) What are you shouting at me for? We'll say that the price includes lunch and dinner. Or should we not pay the mortgage and have them take this place out of our hands? You should be thanking me, not yelling at me. (*He throws the receipt at her and exits*)

Luigia: Go away! Get out of my sight!

(*Aydın Tuna enters cheerfully*)

Aydın Tuna:	Hello, Mrs Giorgio, I've unpacked. It's so nice to be able to travel with a small bag. I think I'll go for a short walk in the garden just now. I'll go down to the sea. I'm hungry, too. What time is lunch? Do you have any other guests?
Luigia:	There's no one else apart from you, yet. Of course, there will be more, I hope. We're waiting. (*Sheepishly*) Signor Tuna, there's something I have to explain to you. It's rather awkward.
Aydın Tuna:	What is it?
Luigia:	It's between thirty and fifty Euro a night here for half board and full board. My brother asked for two hundred from you when he learned you were Turkish. He thought you'd haggle over the price. And you believed him. He's put the money in the bank. And we're really not in a position to be able to pay it back. We're having some financial problems. They'll pass, of course. We owe you four hundred and fifty Euro, but how can we pay you back? I'm trying to think of something.
Aydın Tuna:	Don't worry about it. If I'd been staying in a five-star hotel, I would have been paying that much. What's the difference? You can pay me back whenever you're in better straits. And, while you're at it, don't write six hundred in the account book. No one has to know the real situation.
Luigia:	My God, how good you are! I promise I'll pay you your four hundred and fifty Euro as soon as I can. Definitely...

Aydın Tuna:	OK, it's a deal.

Luigia: Lunch will be ready in an hour. I'll cook the most delicious Sicilian dishes for you. What would you like?

Aydın Tuna: Come, let's go into the kitchen. First, let's see what ingredients we have. Then we'll finalise the menu. (*They exit through the door and re-enter*) Mouthwatering Sicilian-style pasta, Caesar salad, roast chicken and a cappucino. I'll be back in an hour. (*He exits*)

(*Vittorio enters*)

Vittorio: Have you calmed down yet?

Luigia: I told Signor Tuna. He had to know that we owe him four hundred and fifty Euro. He said we could pay him back whenever we were in better straits.

Vittorio: Well, that's just wonderful! We're even in debt to the Turks now. Look, the man lives in Istanbul. If he doesn't forget, we can still tell him that we're in bad straits. He'll never know.

Luigia: (*In a rage*) Go away! Get out of my sight!

(*Vittorio exits cheerfully*)

(*The next day, the same place. Aydın Tuna is wearing sporty clothes. He leaves his room. Luigia is dusting the armchairs. Vittorio is straightening up the carpet.*)

Aydın Tuna:	Good morning, what a beautiful day! Everywhere's so bright.
Luigia:	Did you sleep well? Are you happy with your room?
Aydın Tuna:	I couldn't have hoped for anything better.
Luigia:	Thank you. Your breakfast is ready.
Aydın Tuna:	After breakfast, I'll go for a little swim and sleep in the afternoon. You call it a siesta, don't you, the nap you have after eating?
Luigia:	Yes, Signor Tuna, we do.
Aydın Tuna:	(*Looking at Vittorio*) Vittorio, can you take me on a little tour after four o'clock? Let's go into town. I'd like to rent your old banger for a few hours.
Vittorio:	At your service, Sir. I'll take you around. Don't worry about the cost. Whatever you see fit. I'll give you a knock at four. (*Aydın Tuna exits*)

(*It is the afternoon; Aydın Tuna and Vittorio enter through the garden gate; they are carrying many bags of food and drink; Luigia gets up as soon as she sees them*)

Aydın Tuna:	Hello, Mrs Giorgio, we said to ourselves that while we were in town, we may as well not come back empty-handed. Me and Vittorio have bought some things for this evening.
Luigia:	Thank you very much, you could feed a whole army with this! I'll have to cook you something really

delicious. Otherwise, how will I ever be able to pay you back?

Aydın Tuna: You don't owe me anything. Anyway, I'm going to go for a short walk on the beach. (*Exits*)

Vittorio: Luigia, I've never seen anything like it before. Me and Signor Tuna went into the market in town together. Our shopkeepers are so dishonest! They saw that our Turk wasn't haggling and raised their prices.

Luigia: You could have stopped them.

Vittorio: Really I tried: I tried standing up to the grocer, and you won't believe what he said!

Luigia: What?

Vittorio: "Look here, lad, don't you go sticking your oar in, come back later and I'll give you your ten percent," he said.

Luigia: And don't tell me, you immediately accepted!

Vittorio: Look, Luigia, I don't want to be like you. I don't want to have money problems. Do you understand? And I'll tell you something else.

Luigia: Go ahead.

Vittorio: The man's sixty-five. He went in the sea. He swam, and he swam. Until he was just a dot... He disappeared from view. I was worried. What would have happened if there was a storm? What if he'd disappeared? What if he'd drowned? And it's not as if the sea is calm... It wasn't, I tell you.

Luigia:

Well, what did you do? Did you just stand there?

Vittorio:

What was I supposed to do? Swim after him like I'm some sort of lifeguard?

Luigia:

Oh, grow up! You could have gone out in the boat. If he'd got tired, or if there'd been a storm, you could have picked him up.

Vittorio:

Well, it's easy enough for you to say that. Go out in the boat! What about petrol, huh? They haven't invented one yet that works on seawater. There's no petrol at all in the boat.

Luigia:

Take this twenty. Fill it up. If he goes out in the sea again, you can follow him in it. If anything happens to him, I swear on the Blessed Virgin that I'll skin you alive.

Vittorio:

Why are you so interested in him all of a sudden? If he drowns, that's his business. Anyway, he's a Turk; we're not even the same religion as him. And that way, we won't have to pay the four hundred and fifty Euro.

Luigia:

He's a person. He's our only customer. Running a guesthouse means being a host.

Vittorio:

Oh, really? You don't say, Luigia! I was joking! I've got a soft spot for this Turk, too, you know. I'll buy some petrol and put it in the boat. Hey, when we were at school, didn't they say that the Turks were barbarians?

Luigia: Everyone says things about everyone else. Don't believe everything you hear.

Vittorio: And wasn't there that film? Its name was two women's names. Anyway, in the film, what did Sophia Loren say about the soldiers that were attacking her and her daughter? "Are these Turks or what?"

Luigia: Is Aydın Tuna anything like them?

Vittorio: You're right, Luigia; this Turk is a different kind of Turk. (*He exits whistling*)

(*The next day, the same scene*)

(*Aydın Tuna is cheerful and wearing sporty clothes*)

Aydın Tuna: Good morning, Mrs Giorgio.

Luigia: Good morning, Mr Tuna; how are you?

Aydın Tuna: Believe me, I've been feeling great ever since yesterday. I'll never be able to forget yesterday evening. You and Vittorio were singing such beautiful songs. Look, Mrs Giorgio, we had an art teacher. She used to say that every Italian man was a tenor, baritone or bass, and that every Italian woman was a soprano, mezzosoprano or alto. Which one are you?

Luigia: I don't know. Probably a fourth group: a crow.

Aydın Tuna:	Mrs Giorgio, if the canaries heard you, they would invite you to join them.
Luigia:	Thanks for the moral support. I'm going to sing from now on. It's enough for me if you like my voice. What are you going to do now? Your breakfast is ready.
Aydın Tuna:	I'm going to go for a walk in the woods and then down to the sea.

(*Aydın Tuna exits*)

(*He re-enters a short while later*)

Aydın Tuna:	Is there anything that makes you richer than wandering around among the trees, Mrs Giorgio?
Luigia:	What meaning of rich are you thinking of?
Aydın Tuna:	I was imagining a richness that cannot be bought with money. I was imagining a natural beauty.
Luigia:	Then we have boundless wealth here, what with this garden and this sea...
Aydın Tuna:	I'm indebted to you for that, Mrs Giorgio. For these two days of my life spent in priceless rapture... Indebted to you... Anyway, I'm off for a swim.
Luigia:	Signor Tuna, Vittorio told me something. When you're swimming, you go very far out. You can't have faith in the sea. God forbid anything should happen to you...

Aydın Tuna: Don't worry about me, my dear. Every living thing will have to say good bye to this mortal coil in one way or another. What difference does it make if it is going to be these waters that lead me to eternal rest?

Luigia: Would you listen to yourself! If I wasn't so shy, I'd be in tears by now.

Aydın Tuna: I'm sorry. I won't talk like that again. Anyway, I'm off. (*He exits*)

Luigia: (*To herself*) My God, what strange thoughts he has. Vittorio should take the boat and go out after him. Where is Vittorio? He must have gone into town. For the commission... I'll go out in the boat. (*She shouts from the window*) Signor Tuna, can I come out with you? I really want to go out in the boat... (*Hearing "Come, come," as she exits*) I hate going out in the boat, but what else can I do? If anything should happen to him, I'll never forgive myself. (*She exits*)

(*The next day, Aydın Tuna leaves his room, looking a little dejected.*)

Luigia: Good morning.

Aydın Tuna: Good morning, today is my last day; I'm leaving to-morrow afternoon. I've really liked meeting you and being here.

Luigia: Mr Tuna, can't you stay a little longer?

Aydın Tuna: I'd love to, but it's impossible. Time and tide wait

	for no man and all that...
Luigia:	They'd wait for you though, wouldn't they? I mean your wife, your children, your job...
Aydın Tuna:	They're not the problem. I have to go. I'd have love to have stayed, but it's impossible; I can't.
Luigia:	You even paid the bill in advance. We owe you four hundred and fifty Euro. You had become like one of the family. For me and for Vittorio...
Aydın Tuna:	The money isn't a problem; there are other obstacles. Look, here's what we'll do – if nothing else, let's celebrate our last night – I'm inviting you to that nice restaurant in town.
Luigia:	Thank you, but it's impossible.
Aydın Tuna:	Why?
Luigia:	Vittorio can't come.
Aydın Tuna:	Why not?
Luigia:	Vittorio is the night watchman at a bank. Four, sometimes five, nights a week...
Aydın Tuna:	Night watchman, but why?
Luigia:	We have to pay off our mortgage. We can't earn enough money from the guesthouse. Vittorio is a night watchman; I give English and French lessons when the schools are open. That's the only way we

can make ends meet.

Aydın Tuna: How much of your mortgage is left to pay?

Luigia: About one hundred thousand Euro.

Aydın Tuna: Such a beautiful guesthouse... Why doesn't it make money? Don't you have enough adverts?

Luigia: No. There's a tourist information office in town. They send customers to the guesthouses. They look at us like the black sheep of the family.

Aydın Tuna: Why's that?

Luigia: They want to buy this place up and build a big hotel here; if we don't want to sell up, they want us to become partners. We are to give the land; they are to build the building.

Aydın Tuna: And what do you have against it?

Luigia: We don't trust them. And they don't send us customers. And we don't have the strength to advertise by ourselves.

Aydın Tuna: And you don't want to move somewhere else...

Luigia: This is me and my brother's life and soul. We'll fight until the bitter end. Until we have no more strength. This land came down to us from our grandfather. We want to die on this land. They'll cut down the trees and tear up the garden just to make a big hotel. We can't be a part of that massacre. Vittorio thinks the same.

Aydın Tuna: You're right. Isn't there anything else that can be done?

Luigia: There is: the florist in town. He's very rich. A widower... He wants to marry me. If I do, he'll pay off the mortgage.

Aydın Tuna: Don't you like him?

Luigia: He disgusts me. Whenever I see his leering face, I want to be sick.

Aydın Tuna: You've already lived through one difficult marriage; Vittorio told me. You don't want to make the same mistake again.

Luigia: Definitely not. My marriage lasted five years. I thought of killing myself so many times. But it would have been a big sin. In the end, they wiped my husband out. God bless them. But you don't want to listen to me all day.

Aydın Tuna: Why not? I want you to be able to get over your sadness. If Vittorio won't be able to come, I'll take you to the restaurant in town.

Luigia: I'd really love to, but this is a small place and gossip spreads. Let's stay here; I'll make some really nice things for you.

Aydın Tuna: I'm lucky to have come to Guesthouse Luigia.

(*Vittorio enters cheerfully*)

Vittorio: Hello, you two. Unfortunately, I've got to be off now. I've got to protect the bank from thieves.

Aydın Tuna: Vittorio, you didn't tell me you were a night watch- man.

Vittorio: Well, I must have forgotten. Anyway, it's not like it's difficult; there's me and someone else. We sleep soundly on our chairs. You can't have a bank with- out a night watchman.

Aydın Tuna: Just be careful. While one of your eyes is closed, keep the other one open. And let me congratulate you on your industriousness, Vittorio.

Vittorio: Thank you, Signor Tuna.

(*Vittorio looks at his sister as if to say, "Come on, tell him." This does not go unnoticed by Aydın Tuna*)

Aydın Tuna: (*Smiling*) What is it, Vittorio? What are you trying to say to your sister? Let me in on it.

Luigia: (*Reluctantly*) This morning, me and Vittorio had a chat. We would like to give you a present. You're leaving tomorrow. We were going to give it to you then, but Vittorio is so impatient.

(*Vittorio goes into his room and returns immediately. He opens the little box in his hand and hands a necklace to Aydın Tuna.*)

101

Aydın Tuna:	(*Joyfully*) How beautiful. Solid gold, too... The pendant is a bee. My dear friends, how can I accept this from you. It's too much. Pure gold...
Vittorio:	We didn't buy it. We inherited it from dad. Luigia, tell him what the bee means.
Luigia:	I won't say that the bee is sacred to us, but it's a very precious animal. When we were little, me and Vittorio were fed on royal jelly and honey. We were never ill; maybe that's why we see the bee as our lucky charm.
Vittorio:	(*Showing his neck*) Look, we have similar ones. We wanted you to have one, too.
Luigia:	With God's help, this bee will protect you from the evil eye and serious illness.
Vittorio:	Me and Luigia believe in that. (*To Luigia*) Put the necklace on Signor Tuna's neck. (*Luigia puts the necklace round Aydın Tuna's neck*)
Aydın Tuna:	(*Very excited, goes and hugs both of them*) My friends, it's easy to say thank you, but how can I explain my feelings? It's impossible.
Vittorio:	I should be going. It's the boss... Anyone who's late three times gets fired on the spot.
Aydın Tuna:	And I'm going to go for a short stroll in the woods. And after that, a siesta... (*He exits*)
Vittorio:	Luigia, that man really is something else; he's nothing

like the losers in town.

Luigia: You're right.

Vittorio: There's just one thing I'm worried about.

Luigia: And what's that?

Vittorio: I won't be here this evening. And you'll be alone with him.

Luigia: You see how considerate you've become! Don't worry, he won't bite.

Vittorio: No, that's not what I'm worried about.

Luigia: So what are you worried about?

Vittorio: Don't you go biting him!

Luigia: You little..., get lost! (*She throws a pillow at him. Vittorio exits smirking*)

(*Towards evening, Luigia and Aydın Tuna have returned from the sea*)

Aydın Tuna: (*Cheerfully*) The sea was delectable. I could have drunk it all up.

Luigia: You should come here often. Even with your wife and children.

Aydın Tuna: That's impossible.

Luigia: (*Wants to expand on the subject, but changes her*

mind when she sees the expression on Aydın Tuna's face) I'll get dinner ready. You're going tomorrow, and this evening should be unforgettable. (*Exits*)

Aydın Tuna: (*To himself*) It's time for me to pay off a debt of my own. (*He goes into his room and comes back with his mobile phone. He dials a number*)

Aydın Tuna: Is that Doğu Kuzey Bank? Can I speak to Michael, please? My account number is 2306.

Voice on the phone: (*Michael*) Hello, Michael speaking.

Aydın Tuna: Hello, Michael.

Voice on the phone: Aydın, is that you? Where the hell are you? I was worried sick.

Aydın Tuna: My dear friend, I'm in heaven's Sicily branch.

Voice on the phone: We heard from Istanbul; you disappeared all of a sudden. No one knows where you are.

Aydın Tuna: Never mind that; I needed some R and R.

Voice on the phone: You did the right thing, but next time, before you do a disappearing act, let me know. And don't worry, I won't tell a soul. We've been friends for twenty-five years now.

Aydın Tuna: OK, I promise. Anyway, I've got a favour to ask you.

Voice on the phone: Fire away!

Aydın Tuna:	What's the bank's cash situation like? It's just I wanted to transfer some money...
Voice on the phone:	How much?
Aydın Tuna:	Two hundred and fifty thousand Euro.
Voice on the phone:	No problem. When do you want it for?
Aydın Tuna:	What's the soonest you can do it?
Voice on the phone:	In half an hour, if you want...
Aydın Tuna:	OK, then. Here are the names. Luigia Giorgio, one hundred and fifty thousand Euro, and Vittorio Giorgio, one hundred thousand Euro. Write down the account numbers and the bank name, too.
Voice on the phone:	OK, got it, now you're going to have to give me the code. You know, the one that only you and me know.
Aydın Tuna:	Bravo, my friend. If you hadn't asked me that, I would have said that the bank had gone to the dogs.
Voice on the phone:	Do you think we're going to forget what our teacher told us? We learnt how to be prudent from you. Tell me the code and we'll do the transfer. (*Aydın Tuna murmurs something down the phone*) OK. The money will be there in half an hour.
Aydın Tuna:	Thanks.

Voice on the phone:	Am I crossing the line by asking if this is a deposit or something for a new investment?
Aydın Tuna:	(*Laughing*) Not at all. Believe me when I say that I hate everything that can earn me money now.
Voice on the phone:	Well, then, tell me about the things you hate. I've been running around trying to find something that will bring some money in.
Aydın Tuna:	Here's why I want the transfer: I'm paying off a debt.
Voice on the phone:	(*In disbelief*) What do you mean paying off a debt? Who's the lucky creditor?
Aydın Tuna:	It's not a monetary or property debt. It's a debt of sympathy, a debt of love. I've got to know a brother and sister here; they have inherited a guesthouse from their family. You should see the sacrifices they're making to pay off their mortgage. I've become so attached to them in the past three days.
Voice on the phone:	I would like to meet these people who you like so much, too.
Aydın Tuna:	Here's some advice: you had a friend; he was the owner of a travel agent in Rome. Tell him to come here. The guesthouse is very close to the sea, and there's a garden and forest behind it. All around the world, there are thousands of people looking for places like this. It's untouched, like a sea of dreams. The owners can do seasonal, even yearly, deals.

Voice on the phone :	I'll tell him immediately. I think I'll be the first customer.
Aydın Tuna:	I have another favour to ask. Be sure not to let the brother and sister know about this. He can say something like he came ten years ago and really liked it.
Voice on the phone:	Alright, I'll tell him that, too; he won't let on. How much longer are you there for? I'd like to see you.
Aydın Tuna:	I'm going tomorrow afternoon.
Voice on the phone:	So soon? Look, let me say this. There's a postal strike in Italy, you know that. The letter from the bank could reach you late.
Aydın Tuna:	That's not a problem.
Voice on the phone:	When will we be able to meet?
Aydın Tuna:	Will I have to give a very difficult answer to a very easy question? Take care, my friend. Say hello to your wife and kids from me. (*He hangs up*) I'm so tired. Let's take a look at these newspapers. I don't know; there's a postal strike in Italy, and I don't know anything about it. Where am I living? (*He reclines in the chair, and picks up an Italian newspaper. He begins to read; the lights go down*)

Scene Two

The stage has become a courtroom without spectators. It could be the lobby of the guesthouse. In the middle, the judges rostrum; in front, the dock; to the audience's right, the defense benches; to the left, those of the prosecution. There is no one sitting in the judge's seat. The judge's voice comes over the loudspeaker. This should be a bass voice. The defendant, Aydın Tuna, is wearing the same clothing as before. The counsel for the defence is wearing a white gown. The counsel for the prosecution's gown is blue. Behind the judge's seat, there is a sign saying "Supreme Court" in large letters. On a panel "The Trial of Aydın Tuna" can be read.

Voice: Aydın Tuna, rise. (*Aydın Tuna gets to his feet. He stands in front of his chair*) The hearing is open. Aydın Tuna is to be tried. This hearing may not be prorogued. There will be a vote at the end. If the white lots are more than the black, the defendant will be taken into heaven. In the opposite case, if the black lots exceed the white, Aydın Tuna will be thrown into the abyss, where he will be gnawed at by centipedes and rats. When his turn comes, he will burn in the fires of hell until he has served his punishment. (*He strikes the rostrum three times with his gavel*) Aydın Tuna, are you a good citizen of the world?

Aydın Tuna: Yes, Your Honour, I've always tried to be one.

Voice: Have you ever killed?

Aydın Tuna: I beg your pardon, Your Honour.

Voice: Have you ever knowingly killed any living creature?

Aydın Tuna:	No, Your Honour. I have not killed, or even injured, anyone. Even when I was a child, Your Honour, I always used to hate fighting.
Voice:	Life is a right, a gift, bestowed by God upon every living thing. No one has the right, for whatever reason, I repeat, for whatever reason, to kill anyone else. Are you sure that you have not killed another living being?
Aydın Tuna:	I am sure, Your Honour. I have no doubts in this matter whatsoever.
Voice:	Let us hear from the prosecution.
The prosecution:	(*A man's voice*) Aydın Tuna, you have declared that you have not killed a single living being. Now think back. Did not a dog lose its life because of you? You were driving. You hit a dog. It was injured and later died, did it not? Now, who could have killed that dog? It was you, was it not?
The defence:	(*A woman's voice*) Objection. I've looked at the evidence screen: the incident did not happen like that. Aydın Tuna was twenty years old. He was with a friend in a brand-new car. A dog suddenly ran out in front of them. Aydın Tuna slammed on the brakes as hard as he could, but, regrettably, was unable to stop. They immediately put the injured dog in the car and took it to the nearest A&E department. The hospital staff made fun of them. They said that they did not have enough time to take care of people and that street dogs would have to wait in line. The dog was in Aydın Tuna's friend's lap, whining

in agony, covered in blood. Both Aydın Tuna and his friend were crying from the pain of not being able to do anything. They asked the way to a vet's house, but it was too late; the dog could not be saved. Now, Your Honour, who is to blame? The factory that produced the car with the brakes that did not work well? The A&E department that could have stopped the blood loss had they wanted to? Or Aydın Tuna? Let me remind the counsel for the prosecution that they were not driving in excess of the speed limit.

Voice: Aydın Tuna, do you have anything to say?

Aydın Tuna: It took me a long time to get over the shock of that incident, Your Honour. Even today, I can remember the pain on the dog's face. When my financial situation improved, I donated a large amount of money to found an animal hospital. I know that it's not appropriate for me to mention that; you should not disclose a donation, and all that... Still, it would not be right for me to be held responsible for the death of the dog, Your Honour.

Voice: Let us hear from the prosecution.

The prosecution: I have nothing to add, Your Honour.

Voice: I am moving on to the second charge. Aydın Tuna, have you ever stolen?

Aydın Tuna: I did not understand your question, Your Honour.

Voice: Have you ever partaken in theft?

Aydın Tuna:	Definitely not, Your Honour. I'm so rich I cannot see any reason why I would want to get involved in theft.
Voice:	Let us hear from the prosecution.
The prosecution:	Aydın Tuna, have you ever dodged your taxes?
The defence:	(*Before Aydın Tuna can say anything*) Objection, Your Honour. The question was about theft. It seems that it should not have anything to do with taxes.
Voice:	Overruled. Answer the question, Aydın Tuna. Have you ever evaded your taxes?
Aydın Tuna:	Yes, Your Honour, I have. Until fifteen years ago, yes, after that, no.
The prosecution:	Why?
Aydın Tuna:	For two reasons, Your Honour. The first was that if I had declared all the money I had earned, half of it would have gone as taxes. But I wanted to expand, to enter untapped markets, to win approval in several different areas. I thought I would open my own factory with what I would have given the government and in that way create job opportunities for thousands of people. The second reason, Your Honour, is what the government does with the money it gets. Most of the time, they squander it. They do not use it rationally, where it is needed. I spend money much more appropriately and in areas that are beneficial to society.

111

The prosecution:	Why have you not evaded taxes for the last fifteen years? You mentioned that just now.
Aydın Tuna:	Yes, that is right, I have not been evading taxes for the last fifteen years. We had become so large that I was beginning to feel that it was no longer right for us to be going against the authorities. I had begun to imagine what the thousands of people working in my companies would think of me. I am morally bound to set them a good example, not a bad one. Also, Your Honour, if the state is rotten, instead of going against it, correcting it is more in keeping with the laws of a thinking mind.
Voice:	Let us hear from the counsel for the defence.
The defence:	Aydın Tuna has lead a very upright life, Your Honour. Apart from working excessively, there are no other excesses in his life. He has never drunk or gambled. Coming to his weakness for women, it is, perhaps, a little excessive, but still within the normal limits. It is acceptable to think of him as a normal person. He has convincingly explained why he used to evade taxes and then why he stopped.
Voice:	Let us hear from the counsel for the prosecution.
The prosecution:	Typical businessman behaviour... He is used to exploiting a situation to his own advantage. Heads, I win; tails, you lose. And the justification just beggars belief. If he evades his taxes, he is in the right, and if he does not, he is still in the right. If that is not contempt of court, then I do not know what is.

Aydın Tuna:	If the state does not know how to respect itself, if it holds itself in contempt, if it does not use honest measures in its necessary audits and controls, what will be the result? Private investment will start to take the initiative, step by step. It will take the place of the state.
The prosecution:	If that is the case, what are we to do? Are we to put the state in the dock?
Aydın Tuna:	It is not up to me to decide on that one way or the other.
The prosecution:	No further questions, Your Honour.
Voice:	I am moving on to the third and final charge. Aydın Tuna, how would you evaluate yourself as a Muslim, as a Turk and as a citizen of the world?
Aydın Tuna:	Those are things that are very important for me. From time to time, I suppose, I have looked upon God's justice with doubt, which is normal, and that is even how it should be because if the power we call reason is a gift from God, it is natural for us to use it in every way we can and, like I just said, that is how it should be. I must have criticised God many times. I criticise myself a lot. What does that show? That I did not accept everything as it was, that I always wanted to find out the root cause, or, in other words, that I used my mind... If God is watching us at the moment, he will love his creature, me, Aydın Tuna, a little bit more because I am guided in my behaviour by the power I have got from Him. I feel that I am a part of Him. I have

not been able to carry out all the obligations required by my religion, but my respect for it is complete and flawless. Maybe as a natural result of this respect, I have never gambled, have never opened a casino or gaming hall and have never got involved in the arms trade, which aims at destroying humanity like it or not. Although I know very well that it adds wealth upon wealth, I never cared for the drugs trade. I was always revolted by all of that. I'll just add one more thing then finish what I've got to say. A good Muslim and a good Turk is, at the same time, a good citizen of the world. Religion, nationality and world citizenship are, according to me, elements that fulfill each other. I would compare the three of them to complementary colours in a painting. That is all I have to say, Your Honour.

Voice: We have deliberated. We are moving on to vote. The white lots have been counted. The white lots have come out on top. Aydın Tuna has been absolved of his sins. May it be proclaimed at all the gates of heaven. May our new member be welcomed. (*Aydın Tuna and the Counsel for the Defence shake hands joyfully. Aydın Tuna suddenly sees that his lawyer is Luigia. The Prosecution is Vittorio. Luigia and Vittorio exit together through the door. Aydın Tuna looks after them in amazement*)

Aydın Tuna: Your Honour, the lawyer who defended me was Luigia, the owner of the guesthouse.

Voice: Yes, we know. She wanted to defend you.

Aydın Tuna: Why doesn't she stay here?

Voice: She's from the world; her place is not here.

Aydın Tuna: I want to be with her, Your Honour. Will you allow me to return to the world?

Voice: Think well, Aydın Tuna, you have been accepted into heaven. If you go back to the world, when you come here again, you will be judged again. And that time, you might not make it through the pearly gates.

Aydın Tuna: I accept any condition, Your Honour.

Voice: Every mortal has one chance, and one chance only to return to life. When you come here again, you will be judged again. Is that what you desire?

Aydın Tuna: Yes, Your Honour.

Voice: We have deliberated. The decision for Aydın Tuna to return to mortal life has been taken. This case shall be completely erased from memory.

Aydın Tuna: (*Joyfully*) Thank you, Your Honour (*The stage goes dark. The rostrum and chairs are removed. Aydın Tuna begins to take deep breaths on the sofa in the lobby where he is asleep. Luigia, sitting on the opposite chair knitting, is startled by Aydın Tuna's wheezing noises*)

Luigia: (*To herself*) He must be dreaming. (*She perches on the edge of the sofa and puts her hand on Aydın Tuna's shoulder.*)

(*Aydın Tuna slowly opens his eyes and looks around*)

Aydın Tuna: Mrs Giorgio, I had a dream, and you were in it.

Luigia: Tell me what you saw; I'm dying to know.

Aydın Tuna: I was running; something was coming up behind me. They were evil spirits. While I was running, I got to the edge of a cliff. I threw myself off it. I'm falling; I'm going to nosedive into the ground. Behind me there is a cackle, "Aydın Tuna, you're finiiished. You're dead." As I was plummeting towards the earth, Luigia, you came. You were wearing a pure white dress. You had wings, just like an angel. You held me by the hand. You're pulling me upwards; I am at your side finally, and we are rising together towards the clouds.

Luigia: Your dream means that our love will overcome every obstacle... (*She holds Aydın Tuna's hand, kisses him, presses against his chest, and leans forward; Aydın Tuna responds in kind; the stage goes dark as they start to make love*)

(*The fifth day, the same scene*)

Aydın Tuna: Luigia, I've been here for five days, and I only noticed today there's a little spring that comes up between the rocks at the entrance to the forest. Someone has put up a sign there saying, **"Diseases Are Afraid of This Water!"** What does that mean?

Luigia: It was Vittorio; he wrote it.

Aydın Tuna: What for?

Luigia: My father was very ill. Liver cancer, he had no hope of getting better. The doctors tried everything. Vittorio was a child; he was always crying. He managed to convince himself that my father would get better if he drank some of that water.

Aydın Tuna: And did your father ever drink any of it?

Luigia: No, he didn't; "I'm not going to follow the whims of a little boy," he would say.

Aydın Tuna: It's only water; even if it does no good, it can do no harm. If only he'd drank a little not to hurt the boy's feelings.

Luigia: You're right; dad would never drink water; I can't remember anymore if he didn't like it or if he just didn't want to.

Aydın Tuna: In spite of all the research, they still don't know the exact cause of that illness. Look, Luigia, I don't want to reopen old wounds, let's change the subject.

Luigia: No, not at all. I've read a bit about it.

Aydın Tuna: Luigia, I'm curious. Can you tell me a little about what you've read?

Luigia: If some cells and tissue in the body begin to multiply in an unrestricted and uncontrolled way, normal functioning is impaired, which, in time, leads to death.

They did everything they could to try and save my dad. He was given drugs, injected with hormones, operated on, exposed to radiotherapy, but they still couldn't save him.

Aydın Tuna: What's "radio therapy"?

Luigia: Something like neutralising the cancerous cells or tissue with X-rays...

Aydın Tuna: Then the doctors should have lent an ear to Vittorio; for example, they could have washed the cancerous tissue with water. Water is a fantastic solvent.

Luigia: When Vittorio hears that, he'll be very happy because he's always believed water has magical properties. According to him, water is the best medicine.

Aydın Tuna: I'll tell him this evening.

Luigia: Come on, Aydın, let's walk to the spring, and drink lots of that water; I'm so thirsty.

Aydın Tuna: You read my mind. I'm parched too. (*They exit joyfully, hand in hand*)

(*Twelve days later, Luigia and Vittorio are in the lobby*)

Vittorio: Look Luigia, don't get me wrong... I'm very happy to have Signor Tuna staying here, but it's just all the gossip...

Luigia: What's the problem?

118

Vittorio: We told everyone he was here for three days, but now it's been seventeen and he shows no sign of leaving.

Luigia: Who's it bothering? What's our professional or private life to them? If he wants, he can stay here two weeks or two months for all I care.

Vittorio: Haven't you noticed the people who stick their noses in everything?

Luigia: For quite a few people round here, gossiping is like drinking water. They want to drink other people's lives.

Vittorio: I agree with you. The town is awash with rumour. And it's that florist that's stirring it. He's livid 'cause you won't marry him.

Luigia: Does he think if I hadn't met Aydın Tuna, I would have married him? The disgusting old man...

Vittorio: They're asking if there are no men left in Sicily. Saying you went and found yourself a Turk. They're angry with me, too.

Luigia: What for?

Vittorio: I'm a night watchman; I leave you alone at night. Oh, the florist's assistant had plenty to say on that score. I could have killed the bastard.

Luigia:	Leave it, Vittorio. Sticks and stones... Let them think what they want. I'm the important one for you, aren't I?
Vittorio:	No doubt about it... A hundred florists wouldn't make one Aydın Tuna. If I was in your shoes, I would have done exactly the same thing. Anyway, I should go now; I mustn't be late. (*He exits; Aydın Tuna enters*)
Aydın Tuna:	Luigia, do you have any idea when I'm going to leave?
Luigia:	The day you go will be the blackest day of my life. Why can't you stay here forever? Let's start a new life.
Aydın Tuna:	If the genie of the lamp asked me to make a wish, I would wish to stay by your side forever, but where can you find a genie? My time is running out; I can't make up my mind. Why do I love it here so much? (*He hugs Luigia and exits*)

(*Ten days later... Vittorio enters sulkily*)

Luigia:	What's wrong, Vittorio?
Vittorio:	We're in the calm before the storm. The florist isn't wasting any time. He's saying that this Aydın Tuna is on the run. That he escaped from Turkey and came here as he was about to get caught...
Luigia:	So what's he on the run for? Does he have a theory about that, too?

Vittorio:	Luigia, you say that, but when you think about it objectively, there's a whole load of doubts.
Luigia:	What, for example?
Vittorio:	Mr Tuna has been here about a month.
Luigia:	(*Interrupting him*) Twenty-seven days, actually.
Vittorio:	OK then, call it twenty-seven days. And in all that time, he has not called anyone, not even once. His mobile always stays silent. I noticed where he left it, and it hasn't budged. He told me he was married and had two children. Wouldn't you phone your family at least once? And they haven't called him at all either, have they? You should know; you spend more time with him than I do.
Luigia:	No, they haven't called him, and he hasn't called them.
Vittorio:	And one more thing... Doesn't he have a job? How long's his holiday going to last?
Luigia:	He might be retired. At sixty-five, he could be.
Vittorio:	And what do you think about the way he spends his money? He's definitely not one to ask the price of anything. When he's going to buy something, he hands over his credit card, just glances at the amount and then signs.
Luigia:	Maybe he's very rich and doesn't care.

Vittorio:	Let's not kid ourselves, Luigia. You know that rich people are stingier and haggle more. Generosity is the luxury of the middle class. Isn't that so?
Luigia:	I don't know. And I don't want to know. I had a five-year marriage from hell. Then I lived empty-hearted for another five years. Aydın Tuna is a fantastic man for me. A prince... I'll love him whether he leaves or not. Do you understand? And that brute of a florist should know that, too. Anyway, I'm going to cook. Aydın will be coming back from his walk soon and he'll be hungry... (*She exits, her head held high*)

(*Ten days later, Luigia is touching her stomach with her left hand*)

Luigia:	Did you hear what your uncle said, my child? But I don't care about anything. I just don't want them to do anything bad to your father... That's all I'm afraid of. He's been here for a month and I don't want him to go. I love him so much, maybe even more than you. (*She exits*)
Aydın Tuna:	(*Enters, there is no one in the lobby. To himself*) It's been a month; no, I've been here for forty-two days. Two months since I left Istanbul. And still the pain hasn't started. What should I do? Can I really leave this paradise and go somewhere else? How can I explain my illness to Luigia? (*He exits*)
Vittorio:	(*Enters deep in thought with two letters in his hand*) I don't believe it; two letters have come from a bank in Rome. Aydın Tuna has transferred one hundred thousand Euro to me, and one hundred and fifty

thousand to Luigia. The money was sent from a bank in Switzerland. The transfer date is Aydın Tuna's second day in our guesthouse. So why is he sending us so much money? He probably realised that he was going to be caught. He understood that they were going to seize his money. But why didn't he tell us? What sort of a way is that to behave? I take my hat off to anyone who can understand this Aydın Tuna. I won't let on to Luigia for the moment that this money has come. She's so naïve. She'd take the money and return it to where it came from. Ah, if only this money was ours... The mortgage would be paid off; we could repair the guesthouse; I could even start university. If the police catch Aydın Tuna, will we have to return this money? I'm not going to. I'll withdraw it and leave Italy. I'll live in another country, but I'm not going to give one hundred thousand Euro back. (*He exits*)

(*Luigia and Vittorio enter*)

Vittorio: The florist has a message.

Luigia: (*Curious*) What does he have to say?

Vittorio: You're not putting the guesthouse on the market. You're not selling the land. You don't want to be a partner, either. You've made three of the monthly repayments on the mortgage, but what's going to happen to the rest? That's what he said...

Luigia: What's it to him?

Vittorio: If we think like him, then the reason for all of this is that Turk. If we can't come to an agreement, he says he's going to turn Aydın Tuna in.

Luigia: What is Aydın supposed to have done? How does the florist know?

Vittorio: He says that Aydın robbed a bank or a big institution and then went on the run. Then, of course, he smuggled the money to Switzerland. His credit card is from a Swiss bank...

Luigia: Well why did he come to Sicily, then? If his money is in Switzerland, why not live there?

Vittorio: I asked the same thing. He says that it's easy to find people in Switzerland. And if they can find them, they can catch them. And who would think of Sicily, let alone this village?

Luigia: Let's say that you accept and we sell the guesthouse. How can we be sure he won't turn Aydın in after that? The man's a complete swine.

Vittorio: He said he wanted to marry you.

Luigia: You see? Look, Vittorio, I don't believe Aydın's a conman or a fake. How can you tell?

Vittorio: Luigia, there's proof. I didn't want to tell you so as not to upset you.

Luigia: (*Yelling*) Is there something you're hiding from me?

Vittorio:	Not really. Look, here's what the florist did. He called the Turkish Embassy in Rome. The person on the other end spoke very good Italian, but he was obviously a Turk.
Luigia:	Get to the point, what did the florist say?
Vittorio:	He said to the person on the other end of the phone, "Do you know a Turk called Aydın Tuna?"
Luigia:	(*Gasping*) And what did he say?
Vittorio:	He said, "Of course I know him; the whole of Turkey is wondering where he is; the whole of Turkey is looking for him," and then asked who was calling.
Luigia:	And what did the florist do? Did he turn him in?
Vittorio:	No, he said "just a moment" and hung up.
Luigia:	How do we know he called anyone? Is there any proof?
Vittorio:	(*Sighing*) There is; when he made the call, the headmaster and Signor Alberto from the local council were around. The headmaster told his daughter at lunchtime. And, as you know, I'm going out with her. Maria told me.
Luigia:	Well, what does he want, this cracked florist?
Vittorio:	Here are his conditions: he'll pay off the mortgage, he'll buy the guesthouse from us at a good price,

	he'll deposit the money in cash in your and my bank accounts but Aydın Tuna has to leave town, leave Italy and never come back or else he'll turn him in.

Luigia: The utter bastard... The devil in me says to take me shotgun and pump that oaf full of lead.

Vittorio: Don't even think about it. How is that going to help? I say that we talk to Aydın Tuna; let him tell us what he's done.

Luigia: OK, Vittorio, let's think, you've no idea how much my head has started to hurt. Ask the florist for a grace period. We've got a lot of thinking to do. (*They exit*)

(*Aydın Tuna enters*)

Aydın Tuna: (*To himself*) How can I leave this place? And more importantly, how can I live far from Luigia? When I'm walking in the forest, I think about her; when I'm swimming in the sea, I look for her next to me or in the boat. At night, if she doesn't sleep with her head on my shoulder, I'm almost jealous of her pillow. Luigia gives me in abundance a love that I had not been able to get from anyone for years. To find love when you're sixty-five... What a strange stroke of fortune... Yet somehow I haven't been able to tell her how much I love her. It's difficult for me to talk about anything apart from work. My feelings always stayed in the background. Before I go, I'll tell Luigia I really, really love her. I'll say it exactly like that. And my illness? How am I going to explain that? And what if she starts to cry, how will I cope? (*He exits*)

Vittorio:

(*Enters, deep in thought*) You just can't understand this society. The florist told everyone Tuna was on the run, and now they're all on his side. The butcher said to me yesterday, "Look, Vittorio, it makes no difference if they're Italian or Turkish police; we'll hide Aydın Tuna. Why the hell are we going to turn him in? The man sought refuge with us. The Mafia was born here. Everyone in this town, even the women, is a one hundred percent real man." As Vittorio, I was proud to be a Sicilian. Bravo. So there are a lot of manly men in this neck of the woods. That damned florist phones the Turkish Embassy and says the whole of Turkey is wondering where Aydın Tuna is, the whole of Turkey is looking for him. That damned florist spread the word all round the town. Apart from Aydın Tuna, there's no one left who hasn't heard. The Turkish government has put a price on his head but no one knows how much it is. But I tell you, it's a high one. The grocer's son says whatever happens, good character should come before money. Turning in a man who's seeking sanctuary with us breaks omertà. Neither the Italian police nor the Turkish police should try to ask us to hand over Aydın Tuna. As if they're angels themselves...

That Aydın Tuna has definitely got something about him. Everyone who talks to him seems to fall under his spell. He says the odd Italian word here and there. It's as if he doesn't care about the world around him. He's been here for two months. He gets up early every morning. He goes for a walk, sometimes for a run. Then a breakfast fit for a king. Then he goes to the beach. With my sister in tow... When he comes back from the beach, lunch and then a siesta... A stroll in the woods before it gets dark. Luigia is head over heels in love with this Turk. I'm really upset. When they catch him, what will my sister be like?

And another thing... Aydın Tuna drinks my magical water every day. He congratulated me for having discovered it.

I don't know what we'll do with two hundred and fifty Euro. My sister doesn't know anything about it. You just can't work this Aydın Tuna out. Shouldn't he be the one explaining why he had that money sent to us? Well, if he's not going to say anything, then neither am I. He never talks about himself; if we bring up the subject of work or his family, he starts sulking and makes it clear he's irritated. He's such a strange character. (*He exits*)

Luigia:

(*Enters. Holding her stomach with her left hand*) I don't know what I'm going to do, my beautiful baby. The whole town says your father is an outlaw. I don't believe he's done anything bad. Your father came here for three days as a tourist. I liked him as soon as I set eyes on him. On the third night, he had a dream, and in that dream I was an angel and saved him while he was falling from a cliff. That night, me and your father made love. I really wanted him. I didn't use any protection and he was in no state to think about using it, either. From that moment, I was his forever. I had my first orgasm with him. I couldn't tell him that, though; I was too embarrassed. One day, I'll have to tell him. He has a right to know. (*Vittorio enters*)

Vittorio: What's up, Luigia? You're not talking to yourself again, are you?

Luigia: No, I was just thinking out loud. What happened? Did you ask the florist for a grace period?

Vittorio: He says what if he escapes? Trying to find someone in this huge Italy would be like trying to find a needle in a haystack. That's why he can't wait much longer. He's spread the gossip round the whole town. Aydın Tuna is on the run from the law; Luigia and her brother, Vittorio, are hiding him...

Luigia: If he's stolen anything, my Aydın'll have stolen from a thief; if he's conned anyone, he'll have conned a conman. The greengrocer's stupid wife, that painted Jezebel, says, "of course he won't haggle; Mr Moneybags Aydın Tuna's easy come, easy go." Idiots!

Vittorio: Don't upset yourself, Luigia.

Luigia: Look at the mess Italy's in. How many people are there left who haven't got their finger in some pie or other that they shouldn't have it in? And then there's Aydın Tuna, a Turk; suddenly, everyone's become so squeaky clean in front of him as if butter wouldn't melt. Everyone's so honourable all of a sudden, but, God, what honour, what honour, if you take it to market, it's not worth a fig...

Vittorio: Let it lie, Luigia, I know it's not easy. Talk to him this evening...

Luigia:	I'll talk to him tomorrow. He's in better spirits in the morning. Let's say that Aydın gave himself up to the official authorities and they sent him to Turkey. What would happen then? He'd go to prison. What can we do if there's no other solution? Let's say that I go to Turkey. To be near him... I'd visit him in prison; I'd take him food and stuff like that; I'd cheer him up.
Vittorio:	Doesn't he have a family? Isn't it up to them to do that?
Luigia:	He's been here for weeks; he hasn't phoned anyone and no one's phoned him. If you ask me, I don't think he has anything to do with his family anymore.
Vittorio:	Nor his family with him... Wife, kids... It's all just hot air. I'm off; I'm fed up with being a night watchman (*He exits*)

(*Luigia and Aydın Tuna. Luigia is sitting on the sofa knitting. Aydın Tuna is flicking through an Italian newspaper. Luigia is stealing glances at Aydın Tuna from time to time. It is as if she wants to find the opportune moment to say something*)

Luigia:	Listen, Aydın, I've got something to tell you.
Aydın Tuna:	(*Laughing*) Why just something? Tell me anything! Tell me everything!
Luigia:	Alright, darling. I want to learn Turkish.

Aydın Tuna:	(*Shocked*) Turkish? Why on earth do you want to learn Turkish?
Luigia:	You know it; I want to know it, too.
Aydın Tuna:	But I am Turkish; it's natural for me to know it! What good is Turkish to you?
Luigia:	Well, you're not Italian, but you've got an Italian newspaper in your hand. Why are you trying to learn Italian? Why do you sometimes ask me some words?
Aydın Tuna:	It's not the same thing; I'm in Italy at the moment. You don't live in Turkey...
Luigia:	What if I go to Turkey one day? If you have to return to your country one day, I want to be near you.
Aydın Tuna:	At this stage, or, I don't know, in this situation, I don't want to be in Turkey; I don't even like thinking about it. If I leave here one day, Spain or Portugal are the places I most want to go to.
Luigia	You don't want to have me with you in Spain, do you? Of course, the girls over there are God only knows how beautiful. And they're all so flirtatious. You're tired of me, aren't you?
Aydın Tuna:	Of course I don't want to have you with me in Spain! I want you have you with me everywhere! Silly girl, without you, nowhere would be worth living; you can be sure of that.

Luigia:	Well, if that's what you say... I want to be at your side forever, too, but if that isn't possible, then what can we do? I'll still be near you.
Aydın Tuna:	Well, that's a deal, then; come, let's go to bed.
Luigia:	But I want to learn Turkish.
Aydın Tuna:	Alright then, your wish is my command. Within the week, I'll have a box full of books, videos and CDs to teach you Turkish sent over to you from England. Your birthday present...
Luigia:	They aren't too expensive, are they? There is no need for a box full. One is enough. You shouldn't spend your money like that.
Aydın Tuna:	Don't worry about it; it doesn't matter how much it costs. Don't think about the money... I'll take a quick look round the garden and turn off the lights; then let's go to bed, OK?
Luigia:	(*Obediently*) Alright, darling. (*Aydın Tuna exits. To herself*) He didn't really object to me learning Turkish. And he wants me to be with him. He's going to go to Spain. Well, I suppose it's better than him getting caught and going to prison. How can I tell him how much I love him? How am I going to explain to him that he's got a child? I know, I'll write him a letter and leave it on the bed. Tomorrow, everything's clearer in the morning... (*She exits*)

(*Aydın Tuna enters*)

132

Aydın Tuna :	(*To himself*) Luigia is such a pure and decent person. I would have liked to have shared many years with her. It's very difficult, impossible to tell her that my life's been foreshortened. I know, I'll write her a letter. That's what I'll do. I'll write it before I go to Spain, and I'll give it to Vittorio to give to her at the airport. (*He exits*)

(*The next day, Luigia is tidying up. Aydın Tuna enters and hugs Luigia*)

Aydın Tuna:	You know, Luigia, I've been here for weeks; I'm completely divorced from Istanbul.
Luigia:	Do you miss Istanbul?
Aydın Tuna:	No, not at all. There is no reason to miss it. Anyway, I'm going for a walk in the wood.
Luigia:	When you come back, I'll give you some of that cake made with royal jelly that you love so much.
Aydın Tuna:	Luigia, there's no one else like you, you're my one and only...
Luigia:	You're my one and only, too.

(*Aydın Tuna exits*)

Luigia:	(*To herself*) Why is he having the books for me to learn Turkish sent over from London? Why not Istanbul? It's as if he's angry with his own country. Maybe he doesn't want anyone to know where he is. Anyway, I'll make that cake and write that letter.

(From outside, the noise of a car can be heard; Vittorio enters, out of breath; while he is panting, he is not in a condition to be able to speak.)

Luigia: (*Worried*) What's happened?

Vittorio: (*Vittorio tries to tell her something with gestures as in the parlour game, charades.*)

Luigia: It's about Aydın Tuna, isn't it?... Yes, it's about him... Good news or bad news?... Good... But what, what? (*Vittorio makes a gesture meaning rich*) Is he very rich? What's going on? Innocent and very rich at the same time? Wait Vittorio, relax, I'll get you some water. Seeing it's good news, it can wait a little. (*She gives Vittorio a glass of water*)

Vittorio: You'll be surprised at what I'm going to say. The florist snitched on Aydın Tuna, but he ended up with egg on his face. Tuna has turned out to be one of the wealthiest men in Europe.

Luigia :   (*As if she does not believe it and it is all a dream*) Well, then, what is he looking for in this town? Vittorio, please start from the beginning. I'm confused. I'm excited. Aydın's not going to go to prison, is he?

Vittorio: What are you talking about jail? The man's an industry mogul... In Turkey they called him the little emperor.

Luigia: (*As if begging*) Please tell me more. I'm dying to know.

Vittorio:	(*As if giving an order*) Well, how can I continue if you keep interrupting me?
Luigia:	I won't open my mouth, on the Blessed Virgin. Come on, you know you're my favourite brother.
Vittorio:	OK, listen, then... you know that travel agency next door to the florist? Well, Aydın Tuna called them this morning.
Luigia:	(*Nervously*) Why? Is he going somewhere?
Vittorio:	He asked about flights to Spain out of Brindisi, Rome or Milan. And that tart who works there immediately passed on the news to the florist. To stop the great escape. The florist got the jitters thinking Aydın Tuna would hop on a plane and disappear without a trace, so he found the number of the Ministry of the Interior in Ankara from God only knows where and called them. Anyway, there wasn't anyone there who knew Italian. So they said, "Let's speak English," but the florist's English is a joke. Still, he somehow managed to string a few words together. And he asked how much the reward was. There was mention of a million Euro, but it's not clear if the person from the Ministry was having a joke or if she misunderstood. Then she said it couldn't be done over the phone, send a fax. We don't take tip offs over the phone seriously.
Luigia:	What did the bastard do? Did he send a fax?
Vittorio:	Of course, he wrote some things to the girl. And he said he wanted his one million Euro.

Luigia: And what did the people in Ankara do when they got the fax?

Vittorio: I don't know all the details, but, according to what I managed to find out, Aydın Tuna owns some companies, and, of course, they have an HQ. The Ministry of the Interior informed the HQ that a fax had arrived.

Luigia: Well, don't they know where Aydın Tuna is?

Vittorio: You see, that's the interesting thing about it. No one knew where Aydın Tuna was, and they were all worried.

Luigia: And then?...

Vittorio: Then, and I've no idea how, the Turks informed our Ministry of the Interior in Rome, and some people from there called Umberto, our mayor, and asked if there was a Turk by the name of Aydın Tuna in the town. And you wouldn't believe it, but he said that there was and that he had been here for almost two months and that we had our suspicions about him! They yelled at him down the phone, "are you crazy?" They told him a few things about Aydın Tuna. They asked who the idiot who sent the fax was.

Luigia: And then? What did they say about Aydın?

Vittorio: He's got lots of factories and banks. Some say a hundred factories; others say sixty-five.

Luigia: Don't worry about that, where's his wife? Why did he leave Istanbul without telling anyone?

Vittorio: No one really knows. His marriage was on the rocks, anyway. One day, towards evening, he left the company HQ and hopped on a plane. That was three months ago. They investigated and found that he flew to London that night then went to Paris and then Vienna, but then they lost the scent.

Luigia: But, Vittorio, why did he come to Italy and why did he choose our town?

Vittorio: That's something that only Aydın Tuna knows. And he never talks about anything personal. Anyway, never mind, the important thing is that he's staying here. Ah, just wait, I almost forgot. There is an evening newspaper in Istanbul. This piece of news is going to appear in it; tomorrow, of course, it will have hit the morning papers. Guesthouse Luigia will be famous.

Luigia: Who told you this, Vittorio?

Vittorio: The headmaster of the high school – remember, I'm going out with his daughter – he treats me very well. He was there by coincidence when the call came from Rome.

Luigia: You're going to marry that girl, aren't you, Vittorio?

Vittorio: Maria? That's the plan. Hey, let's have a double wedding.

Luigia:	I don't understand, double?
Vittorio:	Me and Maria, and you and Aydın Tuna.
Luigia:	You little bugger, go away! (*While she is looking for a pillow to throw, Vittorio exits whistling*)

(*Aydın Tuna enters. He is wearing linen trousers and a colourful t-shirt. Slightly frowning, he looks deep in thought*)

Luigia:	Aydın, I'm cross with you; we're hearing who you are from other people. It would appear you are an captain of industry in Turkey.
Aydın Tuna:	Where did you hear that from?
Luigia:	From Turkey, where else? I'm bursting to know. You left Istanbul without telling anyone. Why? Can't you tell me? I'm your friend, aren't I?
Aydın Tuna:	Of course you are; you're going to know everything within a couple of days, I promise.
Luigia:	Alright Aydın, come on, let's go for a stroll on the beach. (*They exit hand in hand*)

(*The next morning, in the sunshine, the voice of a child selling newspapers is heard, "Read all about it! Read all about it! Turkish Businessman. Liver Cancer. Aydın Tuna"*)

(*Luigia's attention is caught by the voice, taking her head in her hands*)

Luigia:	Oh my God! The same illness as my father...

Vittorio: (*Enters running, worried, seeing Luigia*) Luigia, I'm
                        just back from town; you've heard, haven't you, it's
                        the same illness that dad had...

Luigia: (*Crying*) What are we going to do?

(*They embrace. The lights go dim; there is a short piece of music; the
same scene, the Doctor enters through the door and walks towards the
audience*)

The Doctor: Ladies and Gentlemen, what has happened? I will
                        explain. All your eyes are on me, full of curiosity, I
                        can feel it. Once Aydın Tuna's whereabouts became
                        known, for some reason, one of my professor col-
                        leagues from the clinic had no qualms about selling
                        his story to the press. That morning, when Luigia re-
                        ceived the bad news, she cried until her eyes were
                        puffy and red. Aydın was asleep. She told Vittorio
                        to come with her into town. They went to a hair-
                        dresser's in town. For years, her hair had not seen
                        the hand of a hairdresser. Then they went to
                        church to pray. Vittorio was following his sister,
                        without saying a word. They returned to the guest-
                        house. Aydın, unaware of what was happening,
                        was writing a letter. When Luigia saw him, she said
                        pretty cool-headedly and decisively, "Aydın, get
                        dressed; we're going to Rome. Your illness is in all
                        the papers. I'm sure you have overcome your can-
                        cer; there's a specialist clinic in Rome. Please, don't
                        argue, just get dressed: we're going there." He bowed
                        his head towards the chic, graceful Italian lady with
                        her new hairdo and who he somehow hadn't been
                        able to tell how much he loved her and said, "OK.
                        But if I really have fifteen or twenty days left to

live, I'll not come back here; I'll go to Spain."
Luigia told him that whatever he wanted was fine
by her, but she didn't neglect to put her own pass-
port in her bag because she wasn't in the mood to
let Aydın travel to Madrid alone.

Now, Ladies and Gentlemen, do you believe in
miracles? I've started to. They analysed Aydın from
head to toe in that clinic. Test after test, and the
results were clean as a whistle, spotless like white
clouds and in the end, "Good bye," they said, "Go
home and write your memoirs. Be sure to tell the
world how you hobbled this cancer; tell the world
so that other sufferers can be sure in their hearts and
minds, so that they can know that, before this
deadly filth has time to overwhelm them, they can
strike a blow, they can step out into the light.
Just like Aydın Tuna..."

Yes, the doctors saw Aydın Tuna off with words like
these and with hugs. Aydın Tuna, with the air of a
hero who has won a decisive battle, returned to the
town with a rightly proud Luigia on his arm. The
whole town – the people, their cats, their dogs –
was at the bus station. I will not be able to continue
without mentioning one other thing: the town or-
chestra. How beautifully they were playing and
singing in honour of Aydın. Let our old teacher Fatma
the Easel's ears ring. Italians are born singing
songs. They had put posters up at every street
corner: **Bravo TURCO! Bravo Signor TUNA!** And
I was in Rome, in the clinic. Before leaving the guesthouse, Aydın called me on the mobile that he hadn't
used for seventy-five days and asked me to come
to Rome. Ignoring all the traffic laws to catch the
plane, which was going to take off in an hour's

time, I managed to reach the airport in my car. (*He exits; the lights go off and come*)

(*The same place, Aydın Tuna, Luigia, Vittorio and the Doctor are standing in the lobby. The telephone rings*)

Voice on the phone: (*A man's voice*) Hello, Mr Tuna. How are you? First of all, let me congratulate you on your recovery.

Aydın Tuna: Thank you very much, Prime Minister. I am honoured that you are calling me, Sir. How are you?

Voice on the phone: I'm well, thanks. Mr Tuna, you have overcome a deadly illness. I congratulate you. Are you feeling strong enough to throw your hat into the political ring?

Aydın Tuna: If that's an offer, Sir, then I'm listening.

Voice on the phone: You have criticised us from time to time, even going beyond the bounds of your own mercy. We have listened. Aydın Tuna was up against us. Do you want to take responsibility for the times when you said, "Gentlemen, what you are doing is wrong," and try to correct those things?

Aydın Tuna: Why ever not, Sir? And if I had powers alongside my responsibility, it would be both a pleasure and an honour.

Voice on the phone: Mr Tuna, the Finance Ministry is yours. When you come back home, we'll register you as a party member and then make the appointment. As you well know, the constitution permits us to do this.

Aydın Tuna:

What if we register me with the party in six months? Is there any problem with me discharging my ministerial duties without being registered with the party?

Voice on the phone:

The party's policies are clear. Anything other than following them would be unthinkable. Very well then, Mr Tuna, you are a businessman well loved by all of Turkey today. We'll have you in the party three months after you become a minister. What do you say?

Aydın Tuna:

Thank you very much. As you wish.

Voice on the phone:

When will you be coming back home?

Aydın Tuna:

Within the week, I hope.

Voice on the phone:

Well, when it's definite, let me know. And congratulations, once more, on your recovery.

Aydın Tuna:

I was honoured to receive your call, Prime Minister. Thank you very much. (*The Prime Minister hangs up*)

(*The lights go off and come back on again; the same place, Aydın Tuna is standing at the other side of the lobby. The telephone rings. The voice is İnci San's voice. Aydın Tuna speaks joyfully. As does İnci San... Luigia, Vittorio and the Doctor are also in the lobby*)

Voice on the phone:

(*İnci San*) Mr Tuna, how are you? It's İnci.

Aydın Tuna:

İnci, how are you? How are your husband and children?

Voice on the phone:	We're all really well, thank you. You can't know how happy we are to have found you. I'm so excited I can't speak. This place was left orphaned without you.
Aydın Tuna:	Thank you, İnci. I'm missing you all so much. We'll be seeing each other again soon. Ah, İnci, I read something in the paper here. You're doing a deal with the Russians. Now, what was it for?
Voice on the phone:	Construction materials. Mr Tuna, I have some very important news for you. We're going to hold a welcoming ceremony the day you come to Istanbul. All employees of the Tuna companies, factory staff and office staff, everyone is being bussed to the airport to see you. There'll even be workers from some other factories. We're all going to be closed that day, and as a gesture it will be counted as an unpaid holiday. That's what your employees wanted. And there's something else. Erhan can tell you.
Voice on the phone:	(*Erhan Tuna*) Dad, how are you? I can't tell you how much we've missed you. Çelik is here, too. We've learnt that you're OK, and we're made up about it. You heard what your workers have got planned. They're going to make a carpet two kilometres long. Two metres wide... They're going to lay it piece by piece between our house and the Holding building. You'll come home from the airport. After you've had time to relax, you'll get in an open-topped car and it will drive along the carpet that they've laid. Çelik wants to talk to you, too.

143

Voice on the phone:	(*Çelik Tuna*) You are well, now, aren't you, dad? You remember the letter you left us when you left? Well, I had it framed and hung it up on the wall of my office. Erhan hung up a copy, too. Listen to what everyone here is saying. They're saying, "your father could be Prime Minister if he wanted". (*It is obvious that what they are saying has overexcited Aydın Tuna. Luigia and the Doctor are looking at Aydın Tuna with slightly worried expressions on their faces. Finally, the Doctor goes up to Aydın Tuna, and to the speaker phone*)
The Doctor:	Çelik and Erhan, boys, if you tell him everything now there'll be nothing left to say when he gets home. Put down the phone now so we can start making our preparations, too.
Voice on the phone:	Alright, Doctor. (*He hangs up*)

(*Aydın Tuna is deep in thought, practically in a dream world, looking at the Doctor and Luigia*)

Aydın Tuna:	I'm going to the beach. (*He exits*)
The Doctor:	(*He is clearly annoyed, looking at Luigia*) I'm going for a walk in the wood; I need to have a think, too. (*He exits*)
Vittorio:	I'll go and weed the garden. (*He exits*)
Luigia:	(*When she is alone, she sits down on the armchair, and puts her hand on her stomach*) Did you hear that, my child? Your father is a big man. Even the Prime Minister calls and asks after him. How they

respect him in town. It's nothing but Signor Tuna. I'm very proud of him, but I'm trying not to let it show. (*She sighs*) He doesn't know about you yet. How will I tell him that he has an unborn child? Expecially in this situation... I really wanted him to take you in his arms when you opened your eyes to the world, but you can't have everything in life. Your father is a handsome, good-looking man. He's a prince, my prince, but am I his princess? He's never told me he loves me. I'll be so upset when he goes.

Vittorio :   (*Enters with a piece of paper in his hand*) Luigia, why didn't you tell me you were going to have a baby? Look, a fax came. From the clinic... Is it the sort of thing you should be hiding from your brother? You went for a check up.

Luigia: I didn't know how you would react. I'm not legally married to Aydın Tuna, after all.

Vittorio: You see what it says? You're pregnant. Luigia, I'm happy I'm going to have a niece or nephew. In or out of wedlock, at the end of the day, a baby is coming to our family. Aydın Tuna will be jumping for joy.

Luigia: We're not going to tell him.

Vittorio: What? You mean you're going to hide it from him? He is the father, isn't he?

Luigia: Of course it's him! Who else would it be?

Vittorio: But why? You're going to keep it a secret? But what for?

Luigia: Vittorio, you heard him just now; he's going back to Istanbul. He's going to go in to politics. What won't the papers in Turkey say if they know that he has a love child? They'll throw him to the lions. The opposition will go off the rails. They'll trample all over his political career.

Vittorio: The man is sixty-five years old; he has risen to the heights; what is there that's left for him to do? A career in politics? It can go to the dogs, his career in politics. Let them say what they want! A new life is coming to the world!... What can be more important than that!

Luigia: Look, Vittorio, I've always wanted this baby. I won't spare my blushes; I liked Aydın from the moment I first set eyes on him. I'm the one responsible for the baby, do you understand? I don't have the right to impose anything on him.

Vittorio: What is there to argue about? However much that baby might be yours, it's his, too. You can't do anything to change that.

Luigia: OK, let's not talk about it anymore. Let him go to Ankara, let him become a minister, then, we'll find a chance and whisper it in his ear somehow.

Vittorio: Well, if you don't tell him, I will. I'm going for a walk. Everyone in this house has got a lot of thinking to do. Things are getting ridiculous. (*He exits*)

(*Luigia goes into the kitchen*)

Aydın Tuna:	(*Enters deep in thought, to himself*) Aydın Tuna Minister of Finance, Aydın Tuna Prime Minister, Aydın Tuna President, Aydın Tuna this, Aydın Tuna that... Fame, lies, ascent, sabotage, ambition, pride, dog eat dog... Why politics, damn it... Leave this fresh air, leave this pure water and try to swim in a sea of mud where, if you can't hold your head above the swamp, you'll drown. Is it worth it, for God's sake? It's worth sacrificing all of it, all of it, for one of Luigia's smiles, one of her cuddles. I need to give myself a good talking to... (*Loudly*) Luigia, Luigia (*Luigia enters wearing an apron, worriedly*)
Luigia:	What's the matter, Aydın?
Aydın Tuna:	(*Looking at Luigia in wonder*) Please, sit down (*Luigia takes off her apron and sits down obediently. Aydın Tuna paces up and down, stops in front of Luigia, squats down and takes both her hands in his*) Luigia, I don't want to be a minister. What's politics to me? I want to stay here. With you...
Luigia:	(*Taking Aydın Tuna's head in her lap as if he's a baby*) I love you so much, Aydın.
Aydın Tuna:	I've understood that I can't do it without you, Luigia... (*They stand up and embrace*)

(*We see the Doctor watching them from the door. He goes over to them*)

The Doctor:	Next to human love, all other desires and ambitions pale. How lucky you are to have been able to taste its boundlessness. I congratulate you.

(*Vittorio rushes in with a report in his hand. Without looking at Luigia, he walks straight towards Aydın Tuna; as he is about to give him the report, he changes his mind and gives it to the Doctor instead. The Doctor examines it carefully*)

The Doctor:	Aydın, you're going to have a baby; that's what this report says.
Aydın Tuna:	What?... I'm going to give birth?
The Doctor:	No, my silly friend! It's Luigia who's going to have a baby, your child, both of yours (*Aydın Tuna's face lights up with joy. He has no idea what to do. He begins to dance to the cheerful music coming from the loudspeaker. The Doctor and Vittorio join him. In turn with Luigia and alone... The lights go down. They come back on*)

(*The same scene. Aydın Tuna, Luigia, the Doctor, Vittorio, İnci San and Aydın Tuna's two sons Çelik Tuna and Erhan Tuna are on stage. Everyone is hugging someone*)

Erhan Tuna:	(*Kisses Luigia's hand*) Miss Giorgio, you are giving us the gift of a little brother or sister. Thank you.
Çelik Tuna:	You played a huge role in dad's recovery. The Doctor said so. We are filled with admiration, Miss Giorgio. (*Everyone laughs at the word "admiration"*)
Luigia:	First of all, it's not Miss Giorgio. Call me Luigia. And the second thing, boys, is that your father made me better, too.
Çelik and Erhan Tuna:	(*Practically at the same time*) Were you ill?

Luigia: Worse than that, it was as if I wasn't alive; I was a lifeless, but breathing thing. After Aydın came, the sun started to rise more beautifully, the flowers started to bloom in a different way, and even the birds started to sing more sweetly. Vittorio can vouch for what I'm saying. Can't you, Vittorio?

Vittorio: It's true; the difference between Luigia now and Luigia two months ago is as clear as the difference between light and darkness.

Luigia: (*Looking at Erhan Tuna and Çelik Tuna*) Come, let me show you around a little.

İnci San: That would be great. We want to see everything we can in our three days.

Luigia: Three days? You've only come here for three days?

Erhan Tuna: Miss Giorgio, sorry, Luigia, we're going to sign an agreement with the Russians. Mrs San's going to take me to Moscow with her. We have a meeting with the them next week.

Luigia: I definitely won't let you go before a week. Call the Russians. They can wait another seven days. (*Looking at Aydın Tuna*) Isn't that right, Aydın!

Aydın Tuna: (*Nodding his head*) Luigia doesn't only speak the truth, she speaks it beautifully.

İnci San: Well, boys, you heard. That's what the boss says. (*Looking at Erhan Tuna*) Erhan, call Moscow tomorrow, let them know what's going on...

Erhan Tuna:	Yes, Mrs San.
Luigia:	Come on then. Everyone, get on your tracksuits, we're going to the wood. A red colour will suit our faces better than a wan yellow.

(*The lights go down and come back on again. The same scene, the same characters. İnci San and Luigia are deep in conversation. Aydın Tuna is talking to his sons. And the Doctor is telling Vittorio something*)

İnci San:	Luigia, we've had a lovely week. A week we'll never forget.
Luigia:	You're always welcome here. Next time, bring your husband.
İnci San:	We'll definitely come. And our Istanbul is waiting for you. I'd like to put you up when you come to Istanbul.
Luigia:	I really want to see Istanbul. Aydın says that we might be able to go in three or four months time.
İnci San:	I think Mr Tuna's wife will agree to a divorce. No, no, she doesn't want maintenance or anything like that. It'll just take a little time for her female pride to stomach it.
Luigia:	I'm not saying she isn't in the right. It isn't easy to give up a man of Aydın Tuna's calibre. I think it's all about the stars being in harmony; if they're not, no marriage is going to work out. Even if both sides are perfect...

İnci San:	You're so right. (*Looking at her watch*) Come on boys, come on Doctor, it's time to go.
Luigia:	Where's your car? (*She exits*)

(*Following her, Çelik Tuna, Erhan Tuna, the Doctor and Aydın Tuna exit. Only İnci San and Vittorio are left in the lobby*)

İnci San:	Good bye, Vittorio, thank you, too, for having us.
Vittorio:	It was an honour.
İnci San:	(*They shake hands at the door*) Take good care of our boss, Vittorio. Aydın Tuna was a businessman beyond compare. Through the years, he has become a person beyond compare. Take very good care of our boss. (*She exits*)

— THE END —